Sex Sta
On Scr

I looked down at m
my naked image in the mirror, watching as her palms caressed her perfect tits. She was much bolder than me, because one of her hands slid down her torso until her fingertips reached her jet-black curls. She smiled at me – and I smiled at her, gazing down as my own fingers lightly rubbed my pubis. It felt nice, very nice.

Having slowly crept up on me, that was the night when I finally became aware of my own sexuality . . .

By the same author

BLONDE
BRUNETTE
REDHEAD
SCARLET
HONEY

Blue

SUZANNE DE NIMES

NEON

A NEON PAPERBACK

This paperback edition published in 2006 by Neon
The Orion Publishing Group Ltd.
Orion House, 5 Upper St Martin's Lane
London WC2H 9EA

All characters in this publication are fictitious and any resemblance to real persons, living or dead, is purely coincidental.

A CIP catalogue record for this book is available from the British Library.

Printed and bound in the UK by Mackays of Chatham.

ISBN 9781905619276

Blue

CHAPTER ONE

The cover of the video cassette is very distinctive because it is so discreet.

The illustration shows just one girl, who is not even totally naked. She is kneeling on a bed, her hands on her hips. Her hair is jet black, a wild mass of curls framing her face and cascading over her shoulders. She gazes directly and invitingly at the viewer, while the tip of her tongue touches the glossy red of her upper lip. All she wears is a flimsy camisole, white and lacy. Its buttons are unfastened, and the garment hangs open to reveal the inner curves of her breasts. The pinkness of her nipples can be detected through the holes in the lace. She sits on her heels, her bare legs pressed close together. At the junction of her thighs is a hint of darkness, which could either be shadow or a glimpse of pubic hair.

Take the cassette from its case, slide it into the video recorder and watch as the film begins to roll.

There is a man in a large office, sitting behind a desk. A computer is in front of him, and he studies the screen, one hand tapping out figures on the keyboard, while simultaneously speaking into the telephone which he holds in his other hand. What he says is inaudible because of the soundtrack music. The camera focuses on the computer monitor, the colour graphics of which are replaced by the film credits scrolling up the screen.

His name is John. He is about thirty, fair-haired, and his features could have been moulded from a classical statue. He is wearing a white business shirt which cannot hide the muscles of his arms and torso. The credits end, and the original complex diagrams return to the computer screen. John glances to one side as a file of documents is placed on the corner of his desk. Still talking, still working on the keyboard, he nods his thanks. There is a close-up of his eyes, in which the girl who has delivered the file is visible as she walks away. She is seen from the rear, wearing high heels and seamed stockings, short skirt and white blouse, her black hair curling halfway down her back.

It is clear that John is a high-powered executive. He hangs up the phone, then studies the papers he has been given, glances at his watch, and looks back at the graphs on the computer screen. His fingers dance across the keyboard, and the screen blanks. He switches off his computer, leans back in his padded leather chair, stretches his arms and stands up.

The next scene shows John walking down the street. He is much taller than most of the passers-by; he must be well over six feet tall. The document file the secretary gave him is in his hand. He is wearing an expensive suit, but although it is a warm summer evening he does not seem uncomfortable. He picks up a newspaper from a rack outside a shop, then goes inside to pay. As he walks towards the counter, he turns his head and looks up towards the row of men's magazines on the top shelf. His gaze is drawn to one particular magazine, one particular girl.

It is the same girl who is on the cover of the video tape. In fact, it is exactly the same picture.

And it is as if the covergirl is staring directly at John.

But it is not that which has attracted his attention. His eyes are again seen in close-up, the magazine cover reflected in them. Then the image changes to the same one which was there before: the office girl, seen from the rear and walking away from his desk.

John shakes his head, looks away and pays for the newspaper, then turns to leave the shop. His eyes, however, are drawn upwards again, to the same magazine, to the same girl.

Is it the same girl? The one on the cover and the one from his office?

He hesitates then reaches for the magazine, pays for it, and walks towards the door. He glances at the cover again.

The girl is half-smiling; her areolae are visible, pinkly peeping from the edges of her camisole; and her pubic curls are very evident.

The man frowns. Was this the model's pose a few seconds ago? It must have been. He tucks the magazine and newspaper in with his documents and leaves the shop.

Now we are in a luxury apartment. It is night, and the lights of the city can be seen through the penthouse windows. The camera scans the expensive room. The stereo is playing, and the graphic equalizer is in time to the background music which has been playing ever since the video began. The apartment seems empty, until the bathroom door comes into focus.

John steps out. He is naked, his toothbrush in his mouth; he is obviously getting ready for bed, but from his expression he is deep in thought. He walks across the main room. The lithe, muscular shape which his clothes could not hide is now fully revealed, and his thick cock swings from side to side as he moves.

He stops in front of his computer, where the screen shows similar diagrams to those displayed in his office. Still cleaning his teeth with his left hand, his right hand races across the keyboard. He pauses, gazes at the screen, then lifts the file of documents from his desk. As he does so, the magazine falls free and drops to the floor. He picks it up and stares at the girl on the cover.

Her hardened nipples are now fully revealed; her smile is wider – and so are her legs. She appears to stare directly at him.

John has kept on cleaning his teeth, but now he stops. He gazes at the girl, then he turns his head, glancing at the screen. He removes his toothbrush, turns off his computer, and carries the magazine towards the bedroom. Only when he is lying on his bed does he open the magazine. He starts flicking through the glossy pages, hunting for more pictures of the girl who is on the cover.

He finds her spread across the centre pages. She is totally nude, the lacy camisole is no longer there, and her pubic curls are fully visible because she is now lying on her back. Her pubic hairs stand out in stark contrast against her creamy white skin; jet-black, they have been trimmed into the shape of a heart. Her hands are still on her hips – and her eyes still seem to stare at John, who leans closer to the magazine for a better view of the girl.

Then the camera angle changes. As if looking through John's eyes, the camera moves nearer to the magazine until the page fills the screen. It sees what John sees:

A photograph of a naked girl.

A naked girl who begins to move.

A naked girl who is no longer only a photograph . . .

Her hands begin to slowly slide across her hips, until her fingertips touch, brushing over her black curls. At the same time, she stretches out her toes, her legs slipping down over the white sheet. A glimpse of pink becomes visible at the junction of her thighs.

Her interlaced fingers are pointing down towards her cleft, and for a moment it seems that this is the direction which her hands will move. Instead, her palms start to caress the flatness of her stomach before gliding up over her ribcage, aiming towards the tempting softness of her breasts and the hardness of her nipples.

It is not only her hands which are moving. Her hips rock softly from side to side, and very slowly her legs spread wider. Where they meet, there is now far more than a hint of pink. Her eyes had been open, but now they close and she tilts back her head. When her hands finally touch the contours of her breasts, her lips part in a sigh of pleasure. As her fingers work their magic upon her exquisite flesh, her breathing gradually becomes faster and faster.

She fondles her breasts, gently rolling the dilated nipples between her fingers. At first, her left hand is on her left boob, right upon right. Then she crosses her arms, switching hands and caressing her perfect tits with the opposite palms. Her hands move slowly, sensuously, over and around her flesh, while her body begins to writhe more quickly, her buttocks rotating against the sheet, her hips sinuously rolling to and fro.

Her tongue flickers from her mouth, moistening her red lips. Her legs bend at the knee, and she arches her whole body upwards, raising her crotch up and up until it becomes the highest part of her.

The camera moves closer and closer, but it is not directed towards her pubic mound. Instead it focuses on the girl's face, closer and closer, until her features fill the screen. What the girl is doing to herself now, where she is stroking and touching and fondling her naked body, can only be guessed.

She is breathing harder and harder, faster and faster, her lips parted with absolute pleasure, her eyes squeezed blissfully shut. Then she sighs from deep within, the sound resonating up from the heart of her femininity – the first whisper of a woman who is ascending towards her peak. The sighs gradually become moans, then cries of delight and triumph. Her rapture is clearly visible in her ecstatic expression, and her mouth opens even wider as she shrieks out in ultimate appreciation of the orgasm she has bestowed upon herself.

Her moans subside back into sighs, becoming softer, less frequent, and her breathing begins to slow down. Her mouth closes, and her lips form a contented smile. Then her left eye half opens, as if she is peeping. With her eyes shut, she had been lost in a world of her own, a world she had created herself, a world of desire and self-love, of lust and masturbation. But now she is aware again of the camera, and her expression changes. Her smile of satisfaction is transformed into the smile of someone who has been caught doing what she shouldn't – and someone who doesn't care, someone who only did what she did because she knew she was being watched, someone who was even more stimulated by the knowledge that she was being watched by the voyeuristic camera.

Now both eyes are wide open, gazing up at the camera. A moment ago, it seemed, she had been fully satiated. But now there is a mischievous gleam in her eyes. She has only just begun. That was but a sample of what the girl has to offer, to herself and to those who watch. She wants more, to give more and to take more, far more.

Her face is framed by her long black curls, and she glances downwards, where something else begins to edge into the camera's view. Her eyes widen in anticipation as its domed tip touches her chin.

The rounded head of an erect penis seems to glide towards the girl's mouth . . .

She parts her lips and thrusts out her tongue to welcome the male flesh. The tip of her tongue touches the glans, and a drop of liquid rolls down the shaft. It is saliva, and it drips down the vertical flesh and on to the girl's hand.

For a moment it appears that she is holding the

phallus, guiding it towards her eager mouth – but then it becomes evident that only her hand is there. She is not gripping a cock, because there is no cock. It is only her thumb, only her left hand.

But she keeps on treating the thumb as though it were a penis, kissing and licking at the flesh, rubbing it all around her lips and then drawing it into her mouth. Sucking it in deep, then sliding it out again, tonguing its length, teasing at it with her teeth, gliding it over her mouth as if it were a lipstick, wetting her lips until they glisten, it is evident that this is what she has been fantasising. She has been alone, with only her own hands and imagination for company, but virile male flesh is what she dreamed of, what she craved – a hard knob to caress and adore, because this was the true route to ultimate fulfilment.

Her eyes are half-closed, and she is beginning to breathe faster again as she rubs her erect thumb over her face and her chin and her cheeks, leaving streaks of saliva across her skin. She smiles seductively, and the camera pulls back to show what her right hand has been doing meanwhile. Her fingers are still massaging her breasts, stroking first one boob and then the other. The girl's nipples are harder than ever, even the areolae pinkly swollen. While she continues fondling herself and sucking her thumb, the camera continues downwards, downwards, until once again she is shown totally nude.

Whereas before there was some modesty in her pose, now there is none. Her legs are spread wide in sexual abandon, and slowly the camera zooms in until it focuses upon her cunt. Her swollen labia fill the screen, inner and outer lips fully detailed, wet and slippery with her orgasmic juices, her clitoris shiny and glistening.

Her left hand comes into view, thumb coated with saliva. She rubs the tip of her thumb around the folds of her labia minora, and they tremble at her touch, then she lightly caresses her clit. She sighs with delight, then reluctantly draws her hand away. Her other fingers clench, while her index finger remains straight, and it seems that she is about to stroke herself again. Maybe this time she will slide her finger within the walls of her vagina, using it as a phallus.

Instead, her palm turns and her finger curls. She beckons towards the camera – towards the camera and beyond.

Her hand moves out of frame, leaving only her enticing twat in view. Her secret flesh comes closer, then retreats, then closer again. She is rocking her hips up and down, almost fucking the camera lens.

Then her thumb returns, gliding across her moist clitoris, and her hips writhe with exquisite pleasure at the tender touch.

Except it isn't the girl's thumb which is stroking her pink flesh . . .

. . . it really is a penis!

She is clutching a hard prick in her hand, rubbing the purple glans all across her sensitive cunt, over her clit and between her labia. Her hips buck up and down ever more frantically as she rolls herself against the firm male flesh, and she moans even louder.

The helmet gleams from its contact with her secretions, and she rubs and rubs herself, around and around, her fingers guiding the glans towards the route it must take, allowing it to glide in a fraction, then out, a fraction more, then in, a fraction more each time, then out, until at last it can go no deeper because her hand is in the way, and so she releases her grip, thrusts her hungry cunt upwards, and the shaft slides all the way in.

And she cries out even louder, with even more pleasure.

The camera can see nothing but flesh, flesh against flesh, flesh within flesh, flesh upon flesh. Everything has become still. Then the flesh finally begins to move, and as the shaft slowly draws backwards, so the camera also draws away. But when cock glides back into cunt, the camera continues its retreat, pulling away to show the two naked figures fucking upon the bed.

Him upon her.

Man upon woman.

John upon the girl . . .

His bedroom and the magazine have become as one. He and the girl have become as one. He has entered the fantasy world – and he has entered her.

Their bodies are clutched tight, arms around one another, his legs between hers, buttocks thrusting as they urgently give themselves to one another. They screw as if their lives depend upon it, as if this is something neither of them has done for ages, as if they have craved this moment forever. Their hands rove across one another's flesh, hers urging him deeper within her body, his caressing her breasts and her face, stroking her hair. Then her legs take the place of her hands as she wraps her thighs around his waist, crushing him ever closer, and her hands are free to explore the rest of his lithe body, stroking every inch of his muscular flesh. And all the while she whispers and sighs, pants and moans, every breath she takes bringing her closer towards the paradise of orgasm.

The way she writhes and rolls beneath him, it is almost as if they are locked in mortal combat. The girl twists and wriggles, thrusting her hips up against his, as though she were trying to free herself.

Then suddenly their positions are reversed. He moved one way, she went the same, but then quickly rolled in the opposite direction. Now John is beneath her, she is on top – yet their loins remain locked together, his cock still embedded deep within her cunt.

Sitting astride his supine body, the girl is now in control. She leans forward, her hands pinning his wrists to the bed, and John willingly surrenders. She raises her hips, and his tool becomes visible as it begins to slide out of her throbbing twat. But before it can slip totally free, she lowers herself again, capturing his manhood. Her eyes are closed as she rides him, her breath coming in shorter and shorter bursts, her moans of pleasure growing louder and louder.

John raises his head, his tongue reaching out towards her swaying breasts, his lips capturing her left nipple and sucking it into his mouth, then releasing it and entrapping her right boob, drawing as much of her soft female flesh into his mouth as he can – and making the girl purr with even more divine pleasure.

She draws her hips up then down, rocking herself forward then back, from side to side, his shaft gliding over the walls of her cunt and across her quivering clit. Faster and faster, as her voice becomes louder and louder, until she yells out her final cry of victory and becomes totally still for a moment. It is a moment which for her lasts an eternity, until the internal eruption at her core explodes outwards and her whole being trembles and quakes. The incandescence sends rivers of fire shooting through her veins into every atom of her body, and she becomes totally aware, totally alive.

Then, after another moment, the girl is totally drained and she sinks down, falling into John's arms. His face is an inch from hers, and they stare into one another's eyes. It is as if each of them is wondering who the other is, where they came from, how they happen to be here together.

But this is not a time for questions, there is no need for words. Their communication is on a far more intimate level than mere language. Everything else is forgotten when they kiss for the first time, losing all and sharing everything as they passionately embrace.

They are side by side now, and their loins are no longer locked together. One of his hands ventures down over the heart-shaped nest of hairs to cup her vulva, his fingertips probing her wetness, and her body trembles with delight at his expert touch. Then one of her hands finds his rigid cock, slick from being inside her, her fingers circling its girth before exploring its length. She slides her palm down to the base of the shaft, lightly tugging at his pubic hairs, then caresses his balls, feeling them contract at her touch. Her fingers glide back upwards, sensing the latent vitality deep within, until they reach the ridge which encircles the glans. She runs her index finger around and around, then up and over the smooth helmet, to where a bead of liquid oozes from the slit at the very apex.

While they kiss, while his fingers weave their spell upon her mesmerised twat, she takes a firmer grip of his tool and begins manipulating his manhood. But then his hand retreats from its own activities, gripping her wrist in order to make her stop. She ceases sliding her hand up and down, but she does not release her prize.

Instead, her mouth surrenders his tongue, and she slithers down the bed. John loses his hold upon her vagina, but her hand retains possession of his rigidity as her head moves ever closer towards it. She rolls him on to his back and gazes down at his captive cock. Staring at his manhood, her eyes are wide and she is smiling. She has become still now, her face only a few inches away from his potent flesh. His penis moves, stretching up towards her. But it is not moving of its own volition. Being erect, it was lying horizontal, parallel to his supine body. Now it raises itself towards the vertical because the girl is manipulating his penis, aiming it at her mouth – and her mouth opens in welcome.

But, long as it is, John's penis cannot quite reach the girl's waiting lips. Suddenly, her tongue darts out. Her wet pink flesh laps across the smooth purple head, then slowly retreats. A thread of silver, as delicate as the finest silk, links her tongue and his tool. It could be the girl's saliva, or it could be the drop of semen which had oozed from the tip of his penis. Slender as it is, the thread is like a chain binding the two of them. The girl cannot escape. One taste and all has been lost.

Her tongue stretches out again, licking all over the dome of his knob until it glistens with her saliva. She runs the tip of her tongue around and around and around. Then his dick begins to move back to its previous angle, and her head follows it down. It is the girl's hand which is controlling John's cock, her hand which is drawing her own mouth nearer and nearer to his flesh. Her palm slides down, exposing more and more of his stretched skin, until only her index finger and thumb remain wrapped around the base of the shaft.

Her tongue laps at his length, and her eyes slowly close as her exploring tongue caresses all the way down, then back up again. Her mouth, meanwhile, moves ever closer until finally her lips brush against his penis, just below the glans. She hesitates, draws back a fraction, then purses her lips and kisses his cock. Her mouth glides down the shaft as far as it can, kissing and nibbling all the way, then slowly returns upwards – and her mouth moves higher than ever, on to the smooth head.

But then she pauses, her eyes open wide, and she stares as if surprised at what she sees in front of her, amazed at what she has been doing. She quickly raises her head and looks away – and directly towards the camera . . .

Then she smiles, licks her lips, savouring the virile taste of cock. She opens her mouth again, and with her eyes still staring directly at the camera, her head goes down. She does not need to look at her target. Her probing tongue guides the way, and her mouth instinctively finds the domed head of John's penis. Her head continues its descent, and his shaft slides deep between her red lips.

The girl gazes at what her lips have engulfed, moans with pleasure, and her eyes close once more. She devotes her full attention to the phallus within her mouth. Her head bobs up and down as she sucks in more cock, then releases it again, her lips pressed tight and leaving streaks of lipstick on the firm male flesh. When her mouth draws all the way back, freeing him for a moment, his prick is still a willing victim of her tender tongue. She sucks and swallows, laps and licks, her whole body writhing in pleasure at the oral joy she is giving him – and the total ecstasy which she is giving herself. All that is seen of John is his penis, but that is all the girl wants, what she craves and desires.

It is all any girl wants and needs from a man. She is any girl and every girl, the absolute essence of womankind. She has no name, but every name is hers. She is all female, and all of femininity is within her.

John is nothing; a man is nothing; all men count for nothing. The only thing they have which is of any significance is what women themselves do not possess. But it is something which any woman can have whenever she wishes, something which is hers by right, something to be shared between the male and the female.

The girl rubs his glans all around her mouth and cheeks, both inside and out, between her lips and her gums, then slides it down over her chin and throat, up her face, around her eyes and across her forehead. She is doing with his penis what she earlier did with her own thumb, although this time it is not only trails of saliva which are smeared across her skin.

But having released his cock from her mouth, she now loses it. He pulls away, although she tries in vain to grab hold and restrain his escaping dick. The camera draws back, and more of John comes into view. He has been subservient for too long, letting the girl do whatever she desired. Now it is his time, his turn, his choice as to what will happen.

She had been kneeling above him, and he reaches out to hold her in that pose as he changes his own position, moving around her. While she is down on her hands and knees, he raises himself above her, behind her. She feels his hard maleness between her thighs, and she spreads her legs wider. His prick moves closer – so does the camera.

Just as she had claimed his cock because that was what she had craved, now he demands her cunt.

Her whole body trembles in anticipation – because, once more, this is also what she desires.

The camera continues to close in. On his cock, on her cunt. Probing prick rubs against succulent labia, glans gliding across quivering clit. Purple is slowly swallowed by pink, the shaft sliding in through slick female flesh. Then suddenly it is gone, pushed deep within as if swallowed whole. His testicles are pressed hard up against her vagina, as if also seeking to gain admittance.

He has her, she has him, they share each other. As their bodies merge, so their identities become as one. Everything beyond the two of them has been excluded. They are the universe.

All is still for an infinite moment, and then his shaft starts to draw gradually free from her twat. At the same moment she sways forward slightly, and his knob glides even further out.

Then, as one, their bodies rock together. In perfect harmony, her cunt moves back to welcome his advancing tool.

And they fuck again.

He stretches back, his body upright; she leans even further forward, her shoulders touching the bed, her buttocks thrust up high. His hands are never still, stroking and caressing every inch of her body. Reaching behind to finger her calves and thighs, sliding up over the smoothness of her hips, around her narrow waist, forward to fondle her breasts, gently rubbing her firm nipples between his fingers.

All the while the girl sighs and moans, giving voice to her passion, a passion which becomes louder and louder as his expert cock carries her towards yet another orgasm. Her hips buck frantically, urging him further into her, deeper and faster, faster and deeper. She seizes one of his hands, pulling it towards her mouth, sucking on each of his fingers in turn – as if each of them were a cock, each a different penis.

But having fellated his fingers, she also uses his hand to muffle her frenzied cry of ultimate pleasure as she climaxes, her whole body becoming immobile as though suddenly frozen. Yet deep within she is afire, burning up and consumed with blazing passion.

John has also become motionless, his penis half in her cunt, half out. Her labia are glistening, dripping with her love juices, as if the girl is melting from within.

She slowly turns her head, looking round at him. Her mouth is half open and she is breathing rapidly. She smiles contentedly, then pushes back her hips, gasping as his cock slides deep between her vaginal walls once more.

But instead of continuing to screw her, John withdraws. He puts his hand on one of her shoulders and gestures with his head, wanting her to turn. She obeys, rolling over on to her back, lying beneath him, spreading her legs, waiting and hoping for another frantic fuck.

She reaches out with her right hand, takes hold of his penis and guides it towards her willing cunt. He jerks his hips forward – but instead of sliding his shaft back within her warm wetness, he thrusts his cock over her body. As he does so, he closes his eyes and opens his mouth wide to give vent to his triumph.

A streak of creamy whiteness erupts from his erection, arcing across the girl's body and splashing between her breasts. She keeps hold of his pulsing cock, trying to pull it closer, aiming it towards her face. She opens her mouth, pushes out her thirsty tongue, and a moment later the second ejaculation splatters over her chin and cheeks. Then he comes again, and again, but each spurt is less potent, both in quantity and trajectory.

Sliding her hand towards the tip to catch the last drop of come, the girl lets go of his penis.

Spent, it is no longer of any use to her. Neither is he.

She is his glorious goddess of erotica, he a mere worshipper at the temple of her immaculate body. He has given all that he has to offer, and his libation is splashed across her flesh.

Her hands stroke her own body, rubbing the speckles of semen into her flesh. She caresses her breasts, spreading the creamy drops over her nipples. While her left hand continues fondling her boobs, her right glides up over her neck, towards her face. The girl smears his sperm across her chin and cheeks, slowly, luxuriantly, as if it were the ultimate facial treatment, wiping it to the very edge of her mouth. Her tongue flickers out, lapping at her lips. Then, to make sure not a single expensive atom is wasted, one by one she licks at each fingertip before sucking them deep into her mouth.

The camera, meanwhile, draws further away, moving higher as it pulls back. John is nowhere to be seen. The girl is all alone, lying nude on her bed, still writhing as she rubs her torso and face with semen.

She thrusts her hips high as her caressing hands give her yet another orgasm, and she cries out in absolute ecstasy, becoming still as she climaxes.

She remains still, totally still, as still as a picture in a magazine.

Because that is exactly what she is.

John is lying on his bed, the magazine open by his side. It shows the girl, supine and naked, frozen in the same orgasmic pose – and covered in spunk.

The page of the magazine gleams. It glistens with fresh come.

Then John also becomes motionless as the camera freezes on him, on the magazine spread over which he has ejaculated, and the final credits roll across the screen.

CHAPTER TWO

The credits scrolled up the huge screen, and then the television blanked.

I realised I'd been leaning forward, gazing intently at the video. Now I sank back against the sofa, reached for the forgotten champagne glass on the table next to me, and drained it in a single gulp. I glanced at Murphy, who was sitting a few yards away. The remote control was in his hands. He pressed one of the buttons, and I heard the tape begin to rewind in the machine. I picked up the case and studied the cover, first the illustration, then the back. Murphy noticed what I was doing.

'Didn't want to spoil the plot by reading the blurb before I saw it,' I told him.

Murphy stood up, took the magnum of champagne from the ice bucket, and refilled my glass. He waited for me to say something else. I sipped at my wine, and the bubbles tickled my throat as I swallowed.

'Well?' he prompted.

'It was okay,' I shrugged. 'But the girl was great. What an actress, a real star.'

'Any girl could do what she did,' Murphy said. 'It's all in the direction.'

That was what he always said – because he was the director of the film.

And I was the girl.

The star . . .

Murphy turned as the tape came to a halt. 'You want to see it again?'

'Once is enough.'

'I've never heard you say that before!' he laughed.

I smiled and gazed at the blank screen, thinking of the film, remembering making it. It took no great feat of memory, because it had only been two weeks ago. Things happened fast in the world of blue videos. Since then the movie had been edited, the soundtrack added, the cover had been printed and at this very moment hundreds and hundreds of copies of the video cassette were being produced.

Tonight was the premiere. There were no limousines, no crowds of fans, no television interviews, no newspaper reviews, no publicity parties. Instead, here we were, the star and the director, with a video recorder and a television screen. And we were having our own party.

Although I had just watched the tape for the first time, Murphy had seen it countless times. He had spent hours checking all the original footage from each of the cameras. (It only looked like there was one camera.) He had chosen the best shots, the best angles, from each take. (The long main scene only looked like it had been filmed in one continuous sequence.) Then he had meticulously matched all the tape together into a seamless erotic epic, building and building towards the ultimate climax.

Murphy was a real perfectionist. He never wanted to make the same movie twice, was always looking for something different. Everything had to be exactly right. If he wasn't satisfied with the way we had been screwing, he'd make us do it again and again. That was always fine by me. It was like endless foreplay; and the longer the fucking took, the better the fucking was.

Whenever I saw myself on screen, it was as if I were watching someone else. It was always 'the girl' I was seeing, and I could study her objectively while she fucked and sucked. I was fully able to identify with her, to know exactly what 'she' felt at any particular moment – although I was never certain how much of this was subjective, because I *had* experienced exactly the same as 'the girl'.

There were a few special effects in the new film, trick shots which had been added during the editing, where John's world and that of the cover girl had suddenly become as one. But there had been no fakery when it came to the fucking. That was absolutely real, and so were my orgasms – although I might have increased my vocal volume for dramatic effect.

Originally, I imagined that fucking was the most natural thing in the world: just point the camera and shoot. Who needed a director? But I soon learned it wasn't as simple as that; most people can't even make breathing look natural when the camera is on them.

When I first started working for him, Murphy had always given me precise instructions, telling me exactly what to do with my hands and my tongue. But after a while he learned to leave me to my own devices most of the time. He claimed that I was a 'natural' and he liked it when I did the unexpected – even if it meant having to do a retake because the camera angle was wrong or because the focus wasn't sharp enough.

It was a great life. I was able to fuck handsome guys like John and also get paid for it. Whereas most fucks lasted only a matter of minutes, screwing in the movies could go on for hour after hour. Even when it was all over, I was left with more than just a memory. Everything was on tape, electronically recorded. I could watch myself over and over again if I wished to, reliving the experience again and again.

I must have been one of the most fortunate people in the world because my favourite pastime was also my work – and I really enjoyed my work . . .

I used to love television. The set in our house was always on, and I watched it almost all the time. It didn't matter what kind of programme, because I was a total addict.

The best thing that happened to me when I was a kid was when my father walked out on my mother, because as a farewell present he gave me a portable television for my bedroom. It was a great swap. There were no more arguments about which channel to watch, because now I could choose for myself. I zapped across from programme to programme, a minute of this, half a minute of that, two minutes of something else. When I woke up in the morning, I switched the set on. As soon as I got home from school, it went back on again until bedtime. Even then I watched in bed, often falling asleep while the set was flickering away in the corner.

When I think about my childhood, I can only really remember the TV shows that I watched. I had no hobbies, didn't play sport, and didn't read anything except for the programme listings in the paper. It seems all I ever did was watch television. There was school, of course, but I was never very good at anything. The subjects they taught were so dull, far less interesting than what was on the small screen in my bedroom. School seemed so irrelevant – not like TV, which was all about real life.

When I wasn't watching television, I'd pretend that I was on it. I would be the woman presenting the wildlife documentary, standing on the tropical riverbank a few yards from the deadly crocodiles. I would be the woman crying because her husband was a drunkard, her lover on the run from jail – and because she didn't know which of them was the father of her hospitalised baby. I'd perform in front of the dressing table mirror, repeating what I'd just watched on the screen.

Mirrors have always held a fascination for me; I could never see myself the way others did, because my image was always reversed by the mirror. Right was left, left was right. I used to imagine that I had a double, that there was another me in the mirror world. I would rest the fingertips of my right hand against the mirror, and my reflection would place the tips of her left fingers against mine. We were so close, separated only by a microscopic distance, but we could never touch.

I would wonder about my other self, what she

did when we were not staring at each other – and what television programmes she watched. Were they better than the ones on our world? Sometimes I would position the television behind me and look into the mirror to watch what it was showing, imagining that I was watching different channels from another dimension. Meanwhile, my duplicate looked beyond me at what could be seen on my television.

Because I watched so much television, it seemed inevitable that when I left school I was going to be on television.

I hadn't decided what I'd do exactly. Sometimes I thought I might be a news presenter; other times I considered hosting a chat show; going around the world for a travel programme was another option. Or perhaps I would be an actress, starring in my own series; or there were always the soaps – I could appear in one of those. My decision changed all the time, depending on which programme I was watching. If it was the girl who read the local weather report, I'd want to do that; if it was the glamorous star of some lavish costume drama, then that was for me.

But just like other girls who fantasised about becoming pop stars or fashion models, my ambition was all a dream. I left school without any qualifications and I became a supermarket cashier.

I thought I was going to hate the job, but it was a lot more fun than being at school. Suddenly I found myself out in the real world, and I learned that there was far more to life than television.

And one of those things was sex.

Until I started work, I'd never really had any

friends – except for my mirror image. Going to school had always been like switching the television volume off; the picture continued, but I'd ignore it because it wasn't of any interest. It was the same with the classes which went on all around me; they had nothing to do with me and so I hardly noticed them. Because school was so dull, I assumed that everything to do with it was equally boring – including the other pupils.

I'd been asked out on dates by boys in my class, or ones a year or two older than me, but I'd always said 'no' because I'd miss an episode of the soaps or serials. In any case, I knew why they wanted me to go out. They wanted to kiss me, and I'd watched enough television to know where that would lead.

I also knew what had happened to Mary, my older sister, who must have regretted not staying at home and watching the television that father had bought for her. She'd started going out, started kissing, and had ended up pregnant. There was something else in between kissing and pregnancy, of course, and I knew what it was. Television was my major source of education. By the time I left school, I'd learned the theory of sex even if I knew little of the practice.

I wasn't totally innocent, however; I'd been kissed by some of the boys at school. It started off with just lips against lips, and I was totally amazed the first time a boy tried to slide his tongue into my mouth. But I soon got used to it and enjoyed my tongue meeting another, wetly entwining, lips pressed hard together, teeth clashing. I was happy with that, but the boys always wanted to do more. What I didn't like was the way they tried to slip their hands inside my clothes, feeling for my boobs and buttocks, the way they rubbed their groins up and down my body. I knew what they had there, I'd seen what they kept inside their pants – but it was of no interest to me.

When I was younger, I would cover my face during the kissing scenes on television. I hated them, and they always slowed down the action. But as I grew up, I paid more attention. I learned where babies came from: it happened when a man and a woman 'went to bed' and 'slept together'. That wasn't going to happen to me. I was always going to sleep alone.

Later on, I realised that there was more to 'going to bed' than just sleeping. I learned this from watching midnight movies, which I discussed with my best friend. My mirror image and I would stare at each other, talking together. We got on very well, probably because we always said exactly the same thing to each other.

As I undressed for bed one night, I noticed her watching me – while at the same time I glanced at her naked body. Like me, she was no longer just a girl. We were both on the verge of womanhood. Until that moment, apart from when I pretended I was with my other self, I'd only used the dressing table mirror when combing my hair or putting on make-up or checking my clothes. I hadn't paid much attention to my body, and this was almost like seeing a completely different person – like seeing someone on television, in fact.

I still remember that night, gazing at my nude reflection, realising for the first time what a good-looking girl I was. I studied my breasts, my pubic hairs, and I twisted around so that I could look at my buttocks. Turning again, I ran my hands over my bare boobs. My nipples immediately hardened. Until then, that had only happened when I was cold. But now my whole body tingled.

I looked down at my erect nipples, then stared at my naked image in the mirror, watching as her palm caressed her perfect tits. She was much bolder than me, because one of her hands slid down her torso until her fingertips reached her jet-black curls. She smiled at me – and I smiled at her, gazing down as my own fingers lightly rubbed my pubis. It felt nice, very nice.

Having slowly crept up on me, that was the night when I finally became aware of my own sexuality.

I leaned towards the mirror, pressing my lips to the glass – and against my image's lips. We kissed, and my whole body trembled with delight. My breasts were also pressed against the glass, and my nipples became even more dilated.

After that, I touched myself more and more. I'd stand naked in front of the mirror, rubbing my nipples and fingering my crotch, while my other self imitated my actions. There were two of us, but watching one another more than doubled my pleasure. I would stroke and caress myself until my whole being glowed with inner warmth. My reflection and I would kiss, touching our bodies against each other.

It was all pretence, I was the only one there; and yet it didn't matter because it was so nice fondling my own flesh. Who else could know how I liked to be touched? But sometimes I couldn't help wondering what it would be like for someone else to stroke my boobs, for other fingers to press against the forbidden zone of my pubic triangle.

Most of the girls I worked with were two or three years older than me, but there were some almost my own age who were married or living with their boyfriends, and a few of these even had babies. There seemed a vast gulf between myself and all of them, almost as if they were from another generation. I'd spent my whole life at school; but they had ventured out into the world beyond. They were wiser, more mature, and they knew far more about everything than I did.

Or at least that was the way it seemed at the time. The one thing they really knew about that I didn't was sex – and that was also the one thing which they talked about more than any other.

Working at the supermarket was a lot less boring than being at school, but I most enjoyed the breaks, which was when the others would sit and talk. And the usual subject of conversation was sex. Husbands, boyfriends, lovers, all would have been horrified if they'd known what intimate details of their activities were revealed over a cup of coffee.

Stories were told either to amuse or to impress, or maybe to make another girl jealous by claiming to have scored with a guy that the other was after. Some of it was boasting and exaggeration, I knew, but I wasn't experienced enough to be able to tell the truth from fabrication; the most unbelievable episodes often turned out to be the ones which were true.

I learned a lot simply by listening. I always tried to hide my amazement, pretending that I'd heard it all before, even done it all before . . .

' . . . and his dick was no bigger than my little finger! I didn't even know he'd started screwing me. In fact, I could have had three of them that size inside me and hardly noticed!'

'Size isn't everything.'

'Oh yes it is! *Size isn't everything* is a lie put around by men with small cocks.'

'But you don't want them too big, do you?'

'The bigger the better!'

'Too big and it won't fit.'

'They all fit.'

'If your pussy's as big as your mouth, I'm not surprised!'

'It all depends what you mean by *size*. Do you mean *long* or *fat*?'

'Long *and* fat!'

'I prefer a nice fat one, one that fits really snug and tight, one I can grip really hard.'

'Long is better. So that it slides in further. Good long strokes, in and out, in and out.'

'*Long* and *fat*, that's what you want. That's what we all want. A tight fit and a long stroke.'

'But they can be too big. I remember this guy, I could hardly get both hands around his knob. It was so huge I couldn't believe my eyes.'

'You should have gone closer for a better look.'

'I did! He thought it was his lucky night, that I was going to suck him off.'

'And?'

'It was his lucky night!'

'If it was that big, didn't you choke?'

'I couldn't get much of it in my mouth. Could

hardly stretch my lips around the head. I just gave it a lot of licking, to tell the truth, and used my hands to wank him off. When he came, it was like turning on a shower spray!'

'You got soaked, did you?'

'No, I was kneeling down in front of him and I ducked away. Most of it shot over my shoulder.'

'The worst is when you get it in your hair. It means having to wash it an extra time.'

'That's okay, but I don't like getting it all over my face. Anywhere else, fine. Even if he's screwing me and wants to pull out and shoot all over my tits, fine, if that turns him on. But not my face.'

'That's better than getting a mouthful of hot spunk.'

'I'd rather have it in my mouth than on my clothes.'

'You shouldn't be wearing any clothes.'

'It's probably not such a good idea to strip naked in the stockroom.'

'Why not? I've done it!'

'If you're giving a blow-job, you've got to go the whole way and swallow the stuff.'

'I always spit it out.'

'I always make sure it's out of my mouth before it spurts.'

'You can't always tell when it's going to happen.'

'If you've given as much head as I have, you can tell.'

'Some guys are polite, they'll pull out.'

'Or at least they'll warn you, ask if it's okay.'

'Is that how you know if he's a gentleman, because he says: "Excuse me, miss, do you mind if I ejaculate into your mouth?" '

'How can you answer with your mouth full?'

'If they prefer to pull out, it's only so they can shoot all over your face.'

'No.'

'Yes.'

'Sometimes.'

'I prefer to swallow it. If his prick is deep enough in your mouth, it shoots straight down your throat and you don't taste it.'

'I like the taste. Spunk is a real turn-on for me. If they had semen-flavoured toothpaste, I'd use a tube every day.'

'The trouble with cock-sucking is that's all we get out of it: a mouthful of come – or a face full.'

'Or a laundry bill.'

'You mean the guys get an orgasm, and we don't? Well, I've come with a cock in my mouth instead of in my pussy.'

'So have I. The first time I ever tasted spunk, I climaxed immediately. The only simultaneous orgasm I've ever had. Or almost!'

'But the whole reason to lick dick is to give the guy an orgasm, not so you get one.'

'I do it to get him good and hard. I don't want to make him come, waste all that spunk. I want a good screwing first, and I want to feel him come deep inside me – because that's what can trigger me off.'

'Yeah, but sometimes you just don't feel like being shafted, do you? Give him a good suck, make him come, and you're both happy.'

'There's something wrong with you. I *always* want shafting!'

'When you're screwing, you know how they

usually shoot off too fast before you're even warmed up? Then they go all limp and lose interest? A soft dick is no use to any girl. Start giving it a lick, slide it between your lips; that's the best way to get him hard again.'

'I don't need an excuse to suck cock. I just love cock, that's all. I like to hold them, I like them thrusting into me, but it really gives me a terrific feeling of power to have so much firm male flesh between my lips. I like the smell, the taste, the way I can feel the thick vein pulse between my lips. I'm sure I enjoy it as much as the guy does.'

'I like to save it as a treat – for him. Don't do it too often and he'll beg you for it, do anything for a blow-job.'

'That's right. I can make him come almost when I want, time it to the second. Get him all excited with my tongue and lips, then cool him down. When a guy's got his prick in my mouth, it proves I'm the boss. If he doesn't behave, I use my teeth, let him know that one slip and . . .!'

'Like I said, spunk is my favourite taste. I keep it on my tongue, roll it all around my mouth, through my teeth.'

'Yeah, I've had lots worse things in my mouth. Horrible foreign food, stuff with unpronounceable names, made with who-knows-what ingredients.'

'They take you out to one of those places for an expensive meal, trying to impress you, spending all their money in the hope that you'll spread your legs for them later. I'd much rather crawl under the table, unzip the guy and suck him off. At least I'd know what was going in my mouth, and it would also taste a lot better.'

'You can always vary the taste.'

'How?'

'By covering it with something sweet or savoury – then licking it off, slowly.'

'Instead of marmalade on toast, marmalade on dick?'

'It gives a whole new meaning to the phrase *a knob of butter*!'

'As long as it isn't as soft as butter.'

'Or as fattening.'

'So that's why I need to go on a diet – it's all the spunk I swallow!'

'You say you don't like it on your face, but it's supposed to be good for the complexion, like nourishing cream.'

'That's why your skin is so good, is it?'

'Let's not pretend, it's always the guys who get the best of the deal.'

'If you spend as much time on a guy's prick as you do on the rest of his body, he'll worship you for it. Pretend you love his prick as much as he does, and you can't go wrong.'

'Even just holding it, stroking it, gives them a thrill.'

'Gives me a thrill, too!'

'They can jerk themselves off any time, they don't need us, but they much prefer it when a girl gives them a wank.'

'That's why they think we should like it when they make a pussy grab. And they've got no idea!'

'Yeah, I'd much rather bring myself off than let some guy try and finger me.'

'Let's face it, with men and sex there's no such thing as subtlety. The slightest thing gives them an erection. Rub it up and down, rough or smooth, fast or slow – and off they go.'

'But when they try to rub us up and down . . . *ouch*!'

'They ought to have lessons in school. Like geography; where to find the clitoris.'

'If they use enough fingers, they think it's okay because it must be down there somewhere.'

'Even when they look close they can't find it.'

'And if they do find it, they don't know what to do with it.'

'It's no use relying on trial and error, or male intuition – if there is such a thing. If they can't find your clit, show them. If they don't know what to do with it, show them. They may be dumb, but they can learn. We shouldn't just open our mouths to suck them off, we can talk to them. Tell them what we like.'

'Talk dirty, you mean? Men like dirty talk.'

'They also like you to act dirty. Show them how you masturbate – but use his fingers instead of yours.'

'Or his tongue . . .'

Whenever I listened to these conversations, I became thrilled and excited, yet also nervous and scared. Most of what I heard astonished me. The girls mocked men who couldn't locate the clitoris, but I wasn't really sure where my own was. I knew nothing of masturbation, and I had never even had an orgasm.

The first time I listened to descriptions of cock-sucking, I must have blushed. I'd never imagined there could be such a thing. There was, however, and it seemed that the majority of girls in our group not only performed this amazing act but actually enjoyed it.

I was even more astonished to discover that there was a male equivalent. Just as a girl would draw an erect penis between her lips, licking and sucking until it achieved orgasm, so a male would kiss cunt: put his mouth against a vagina, tongue lapping between moist labia, lips sucking at the swollen clitoris until the girl reached her climax.

The world was far more fantastic than I had ever dreamed.

'What about you?' one of the girls once said to me. 'You never say much.'

They knew. They must all have known that I was a virgin. It must have seemed so apparent that I had never even touched a prick, let alone done a fraction of what they had. But I couldn't admit it, let them know that I wasn't truly one of them.

'You never open your mouth, do you?' said another one.

I looked at her, then looked at the others grouped around the table. As I did so, I slid my tongue over my bottom lip, opening my mouth and pushing my tongue out further and further while I licked all around my lips.

'I do when I have to,' I said.

And they laughed.

They laughed with me, not at me.

I might not have been one of them, not totally, not yet.

But it was only a matter of time.

CHAPTER THREE

'What are you doing tomorrow night?'

I shrugged.

'Why don't we go out?'

'What?' I said. 'You and me?'

I'd been asked out many times before, but never like this – never by another girl.

'Yes,' said Lynn.

'Er . . .'

Lynn laughed. 'Don't look so worried. I don't mean go out *together* – just, you know, together. I'm not a lesbian!'

I already knew that. Unless Lynn was the most imaginative of liars, her stories proved that she was the randiest of all the girls in our group. What I couldn't understand was why she wanted to go out with me on Saturday night. She never had any shortage of dates; there were always plenty of guys queuing up to take her out.

Without a doubt, she was one of the best looking girls in town. She was slim, but very curvy. Her long blonde hair was almost white, so startling that at first I thought it must have been bleached; but it wasn't, it was completely natural. Her eyes were the bluest of blue, her features absolutely perfect. She could have been a model, she should have been a model. But that didn't happen to girls from our town. They weren't models – and they didn't go on television. They worked in supermarkets.

'But . . . why?' I said. What I really meant was *Why me?* Why should Lynn ask me to go out with her? I hoped it wasn't because she felt sorry for me, that somehow she had guessed I never went out.

'Because I'm being selfish,' she answered. 'I want to go out to a club, and I don't want to go out alone. I want to go out with a very attractive friend, because that's the best way to meet guys.'

Very attractive? She couldn't really mean it. The only reason Lynn could have wanted me to go out with her was so that she would appear even more glamorous by comparison. I looked at her, and she met my gaze. She seemed totally serious.

I shrugged, not knowing what to say. Then I shook my head – because that was what I'd have done if a guy had asked me out.

'Have you already got a date for tomorrow?' Lynn asked.

I shook my head again.

'Then what else are you going to do? Stay in and watch television?'

That was exactly what I was going to do; it was what I always did. But somehow Lynn made it sound the worst thing in the world.

'We'll have a great time together,' she continued. 'A couple of fantastic girls like us, we'll have the pick of the guys.'

'But what about your boyfriend?'

'Which one?'

I couldn't remember his name. I'd only ever

heard Lynn talk about him. Then I remembered that the name wasn't important, because it changed so often. Every story she told seemed to be about a different guy.

'The latest one,' I said.

Lynn laughed. 'Fuck him.' She laughed again. 'I suppose I did, but . . .'

'What?' I prompted.

'Oh . . . you know. Never trust a guy. They all think with their dicks – and their dicks are all they think about. If you know that, and all you want is cock, you're fine. But never expect any more than that.'

I said nothing, waiting for Lynn to continue. I knew that she would. She always told the best stories. Of all the girls, Lynn's horny antics were the funniest and most explicit, although I sometimes doubted their authenticity.

'You know that as well as I do, of course,' Lynn said. 'You can only rely on a guy when his cock is hard. As soon as he's shot his load, that's it, he doesn't want to know any more. How many times have you been left halfway to paradise and then had to bring yourself off?'

I nodded, as though I knew what she was talking about. And I did – but only because I'd listened to the girls discuss this kind of thing before. From what I'd heard, however, it wasn't always like that. If a guy did come too soon, it didn't mean he'd leave the girl high and dry. He might trigger her climax with his fingers or tongue. I remembered one of Lynn's tales about being toe-fucked, although I wondered if she remembered it – or had invented it.

I said: 'So that's what happened, is it? Your

boyfriend, er, came and you didn't?' I presumed that was why she'd split up with him and had no one to go out with tomorrow night.

'No, not really. In fact, not at all!' She smiled, thinking of it. 'I came and came and came.'

'Then what was the problem?'

'I don't want to be taken for granted. I don't want them to think they can do that to me again whenever they want.'

'They . . .?'

'There were two of them. Bill and Ron.'

'You've talked about both of them,' I said. Their names were familiar, even if their particular exploits were not. 'But you mean, er, *together*?'

Lynn nodded. 'I met Bill two or three weeks ago, Ron a few days later. I'd been seeing both of them on different nights. What I didn't know was that they were best friends; they've known each other since they were kids. They got talking, found out they were each screwing me, and so Bill decided to turn up the same night I'd arranged to meet Ron. I don't know if they'd already planned what finally happened, whether because they were best mates and had always shared everything they thought they'd share me too – and I don't mean on different nights.'

'You mean . . .?'

'Yes.'

'In the same bed?'

'We never got as far as the bed. At first, I thought it was chance that Bill arrived while Ron and I were having a drink, but I began to grow suspicious when Ron invited him back to his place with us. I'd always gone back to Ron's place for just one thing – to fuck. Ron has this huge old car with a wide front seat, and we all climbed in the front. I sat in the middle. I was supposed to be out with Ron, but Bill pulled me towards him and we started kissing. He began groping me, opened the front of my blouse and stroked my tits, then I realised that there were too many hands on me. Ron was driving with one hand, and his other hand was rubbing my boobs.'

As she spoke, Lynn gestured with her hands, demonstrating what Ron and Bill had done to her in the front seat of the car. This was one reason why Lynn was such a good storyteller. She didn't just summarise what happened, she went into great detail, acting out her own role and even that of her partner, sometimes even including lines of dialogue. Lynn was a very good mimic and could do all kinds of voices and accents. Every time she told a story, she gave a performance. One of the other girls had once referred to 'Lynn's blow by blow accounts – and I mean *blow* by *blow*.'

'So what does a girl normally do in that situation?' Lynn asked, as her hands cupped her boobs.

I'd no idea, but fortunately the question was rhetorical.

Lynn continued: 'The guy is after your flesh, so you go for his. But I had two guys, two dicks, so I unzipped them both and grabbed their cocks. A hard knob in each hand! It was great. But I had to be careful because I didn't want to bring them off, not yet, and I didn't want to distract Ron from his driving. Although, thinking about it, I suppose he must have been distracted enough. My skirt was up around my waist, my knickers down around my knees, and I had two hands stroking my cunt.

Ron and Bill were both fingering me. It was my first experience of two guys, two pricks, two different hands. To put it mildly, I was kind of excited – so you can guess what happened.'

'Yes,' I said, and I could. Listening to Lynn, I was becoming excited myself. My pulse had increased, I was damp with sweat, and I sensed a strange feeling deep within. It was almost as if what she described was happening to me. I tried to imagine having a guy either side of me, to hold an erect penis in each hand, while their hands touched me in a place I had never even touched myself . . .

'That was my first orgasm of the evening,' said Lynn, and she smiled at the memory. 'It was good, but they got better. At first, I thought Ron would pull over, that they'd take it in turns to fuck me inside the car. Screwing in most cars can be difficult, but there was plenty of room in Ron's. Since I'd met him, we'd already fucked in every possible position.'

'I know,' I said, remembering one of Lynn's stories from the previous week. *Every possible position,* she'd said – but many of them had sounded impossible to me.

'Yeah, I must have told you about that. But my first ever car fuck took place on top of one, not inside. Not right on top, because we'd probably have fallen off. I forget the guy's name, but he had a really small car – and a really small dick, which is probably why I can't remember his name. It was night and he was parked in an underground car park. We couldn't screw inside his motor, so I climbed on to the bonnet – and he climbed on to me. But because of the angle of the bonnet, I kept sliding down. So did he – and his cock kept sliding out of my twat. I wasn't exactly getting turned on by any of this, but it did strike me as very funny and so I started laughing.'

Lynn laughed, and so did I. She had a very infectious laugh. But I was also laughing as I pictured the situation she was describing. She was leaning back, her legs spread wide, demonstrating her position on the bonnet of the car.

'And,' she continued, 'you should *never* laugh when a guy is fucking you. He might get the wrong idea. This one was angry enough because his cock kept slipping all the way out, and it was out of my cunt when he ejaculated. That can be bad, because I hate having spunk all over my clothes. But in this case it splattered across the windscreen. I laughed even more, which of course made him even more angry. He zipped himself up, climbed into the car, slammed the door and started the engine. I managed to climb off before he drove away.'

'He just left you there?'

'I didn't care. As he drove away, he switched on his wipers to clear the screen – and spunk flew everywhere! He was driving between two rows of parked cars, and they all got splashed with drops of come. It was *so* funny! I laughed hysterically, thinking about all those people who would find specks of sperm dribbling down their paintwork.'

'Makes a change from birdshit, though.'

'That's right. Anyway, where was I? Yeah: two guys, two cocks. So instead of stopping, Ron drove faster and faster, and we raced to his place. I took off my panties before I left the car, because it was easier than pulling them back up. But that was the only thing I did manage to get off, because as soon as I was inside, Bill was inside me. He knew he had to act fast, to make his move before Ron, and he did. We'd reached the doorway, and he just pulled me towards him, lifted my skirt, spread my legs, then slid his cock deep into me.'

Lynn inhaled swiftly, as if feeling hard male flesh slide into her once more, then continued: 'I thought he was just going to fuck me there, up against the wall, but instead he half-carried, half-walked me inside and into the front room. It was a great feeling, his shaft sliding in and out as we moved. We dropped down on to the sofa, him on top of me, his knob still in my cunt, and we began fucking. But Ron wasn't very pleased.'

'I supposed not,' I said. 'What did he do?'

'He got a can of beer, sat down on the sofa next to us and switched on the television. Me and Bill kept fucking away, still with our clothes on. At least my knickers were gone, but Bill still had his pants on, with just his dick sticking out. But what I didn't like was the way he looked around and started watching the football on TV! Then he said to Ron: "What about a beer for me?" They want it all, don't they? I guess that would be most guys' idea of heaven – watching football, drinking beer and fucking!' Lynn shook her head then laughed.

'Sex and television,' I said, 'what could be better?' I was an expert on one if not the other.

'Sex on television?' suggested Lynn. 'Anyway, Ron wasn't really ignoring us. How could he be? My head kept banging against his hip, and when I looked around I saw that his knob was still sticking up from his pants. So I reached over and took hold of it and began wanking Ron in the same rhythm that Bill was fucking me. A cock in the hand and one in the bush, you could say!'

'Lynn!' I groaned.

'Ron moved around a bit, pushing his knob towards my face. Not very subtle but I took the hint, opened my mouth, and sucked his prick between my lips. That was another first, being fucked at both ends. And it was wonderful, it really was. Two cocks are a lot better than one. The only trouble was, I was so uncomfortable. My neck was twisted to reach Ron's knob, I was lying half across the sofa, and I still had my clothes on. I prefer being totally naked during sex; I like the feel of male flesh all over my body. So I started undressing, which wasn't that easy when I had two pricks to enjoy. It was almost as if I thought I might lose them, although there was no danger of that! The guys helped me off with my clothes and stripped off their own things. I got into a more comfortable position and carried on fucking and sucking.' Lynn licked her lips, remembering, then resumed her narrative.

'We'd ended up on the floor and I'd rolled over on to my front, and Bill was shafting me from the rear, which meant it was easier for me to go down on Ron – who was kneeling in front of me, sliding his knob between my lips. I've always thought that sex is more than just physical, you know what I mean?'

I nodded, although I couldn't imagine anything more physical than what Lynn was describing.

'I know I shouldn't admit it,' she said, 'but sometimes I don't climax; maybe my mind just isn't on the right frequency. It must be the same with you, with all girls. So there I was, two throbbing cocks inside me, and I suddenly thought about how I was being face-fucked and cunt-fucked – and I came instantly. It was more than a physical reaction which sparked me off. I suppose it's like the same way you can have an orgasm without any real physical stimulus. Without a man, without a cock, without even finger-fucking yourself. It's all in the mind.'

I nodded, because that was what Lynn was expecting.

'With guys, of course, it's all physical! Ron came a second or two later, filling my mouth with spunk. I hardly noticed, because I was still lost in my own orgasm. I swallowed it down. Bill was thrusting harder and harder, getting ready to climax, and I clenched my cunt muscles, holding him tight. When he came, it sparked me off again. It was great, really great, better than before. And even the guys must have thought so, because they were watching me instead of the TV.

'When their pricks released me, I sank to the floor, rolled over on to my back, and reached for the can of beer. I drank it down, not to wash away the taste of spunk but because I was thirsty. Then Bill reached for the can and he poured it all over me. I screamed in shock, and he started licking the drops from my body. Ron did the same. They licked me all over, although they concentrated on my boobs. Having both my nipples sucked simultaneously was paradise. I closed my eyes, writhing with delight, feeling another climax building up. The remote control for the television was on the floor beneath me, and every time I rolled from side to side I changed the station.

Comedy and adverts and music and movies and game shows. The guys kept on stroking my body, licking my flesh. "Beer never tasted this good," I heard Bill say.'

'Television and beer and sex,' I said. 'It works for girls, too!'

'That's right. Next thing I knew, I had a cock in my mouth and one in my cunt again. This time, it was Bill's dick between my lips and Ron whose knob was in my twat. So . . . I sucked and fucked again. And came again. And again.' Lynn sighed. 'Shall we go out tomorrow night?'

'But what about . . .?'

'What about what?'

'Bill and Ron.'

'They can cool off for a while. I enjoyed my night with them, but it was just one of those things. It happened, and it was great. We'll probably do it again, although I'm sure it won't be as good. You know how it is: something great happens, but you can never recreate that exact moment. You can never live in the past, you've always got to go on – on to the next orgasm!'

'Yes,' I agreed. At some time during Lynn's narration I'd crossed my legs. Now I clenched my thighs even tighter, feeling an unfamiliar warm sensation deep within my being. I didn't know what to do next: whether to suppress the feeling or emphasise it. And I'd no idea how to do either.

'But I don't want them to think they can both fuck me whenever they want. You don't have to worry about Ron and Bill; this won't be a double date, I promise. It's just you and me – to start with. But with luck, we'll get lucky!'

I still wasn't sure how much of Lynn's story to

believe, if any; but what she'd said explained why she didn't want either of her current boyfriends to take her out on Saturday.

'Let's go out and have some fun,' she said. 'Okay?'

And I heard myself say: 'Okay.'

Knowing Lynn, it seemed I was in for an interesting night.

CHAPTER FOUR

'You can't wear that!' Lynn told me.

'Can't wear what?' I looked down at myself.

'Any of it.'

'What's wrong with it?'

'There's nothing wrong with it – if you wanted to stay in and watch television. But to go to a club? To meet guys? Jeans and trainers and a sweater!'

Lynn was right: I was wearing exactly what I would have done if I'd stayed at home to watch TV. These were the clothes in which I felt most comfortable, and in fact they were almost the only clothes that I had.

'But you've got jeans on,' I said.

'I have *now*, but I'm not going out like this.' She was wearing a pair of denims and a baggy white T-shirt.

'You mean you're not ready?' I glanced at my watch. 'But you said to meet you here at eight.'

'We've got plenty of time.' She looked me up and down again. 'And you need plenty of time. Let's go to my room and see what we can do.'

Lynn closed the front door, and I followed her up the stairs. She was nearly two years older than I was, but she still chose to live with her parents.

'I like my home comforts,' she'd once said to me. 'I like to come home to my own bed – and sleep in it. The best way to get rid of some guy is to ask if he wants to come in and meet my mum and dad. If he wants to fuck me, we have to do it at his place. And I always like to get away as soon as possible. I hate falling asleep with them.'

Maybe Lynn thought she'd been too critical, because she looked around and said: 'At least your hair looks good.'

It ought to have done. I'd washed and conditioned it when I showered, then brushed it dry.

'Other girls must wear jeans and sweaters when they go out,' I told her.

'They do – but you're not other girls. They wear those kind of things to cover themselves up. But you don't have to cover yourself up. You've got a great figure, so make the most of it; show what you've got.'

That was one reason why I wore what I did: because I didn't want to reveal any of myself. I was covered from neck to toe. Apart from my face, none of my flesh was visible. If I was out with Lynn, meeting the kind of guys that she knew, I certainly had no intention of behaving the way she did. I wanted to be as invulnerable as possible, a pair of jeans seemed a reasonable deterrent to probing hands – and rampant cocks.

'There will be a lot of competition tonight,' she continued. 'We've both got to look our best.'

We went into her room, and Lynn closed the door. I gazed around in astonishment. There were clothes everywhere. Packed into the wardrobe, spilling from the chest of drawers, stuffed on hangers pinned to the wall, draped over the chair, hooked on the back of the door, piled on the bed and overflowing on to the floor.

'You could open a shop,' I said.

'If I had all the money I'd spent on this lot,' Lynn said, looking around, 'I probably could. I just love buying clothes, don't you? It's my favourite activity.' She paused, smiled, then added: 'Okay, my *second* favourite activity.'

'What are you going to wear tonight?' I asked. 'How can you possibly choose?' That was one advantage about having so little to wear; I never had to waste time thinking what to put on.

'I usually wear my most recent outfit, otherwise it might never be worn – and so I'd have wasted my money.'

'You wear things only once?'

'No,' said Lynn, shaking her head. 'Some things I *never* wear!' She laughed. 'The fun is in buying them. I love going around the shops, trying so many different things on. You know what it's like.'

'Yes,' I said, although I didn't.

'It's all the build-up, isn't it? A lot of the fun is in the shopping. It's like sex, where so much of the excitement is in what happens before. Meeting someone for the first time, going out with them, the anticipation, the kissing, the touching, the undressing, the foreplay. Then comes the fucking. And buying something is like that, it's the climax of shopping. You don't have to actually wear the stuff you buy, because you've already had enough satisfaction from it.'

'So all these are your orgasms?' I said, gazing around.

'In a way, yes. Except I've had *far* more orgasms than these!' Lynn's dismissive gesture encompassed her vast array of clothes. 'You want to try something on?'

'Can I?'

'Anything. Everything! No, maybe not *everything,* that will take until Monday. Let's just find you something for tonight. We're about the same size, so all of this should fit you.'

I put my hands on my hips, rubbing my palms over the denim, as I studied Lynn's range of clothes. Her offer was very tempting, and I wanted to accept, but I had no idea where to begin. Everything seemed randomly dispersed, tops mixed with trousers, skirts together with stockings.

'Jeans can be fine in the right place,' said Lynn, watching me, 'but not for us, not tonight. When they're really tight around the ass and crotch, so tight you can't even wear panties, guys really go for that. But without undies, you've got to be *really* careful pulling up the zip.'

'I bet,' I agreed, my right hand moving from my hip to my crotch.

'But it's a lot more fun wearing a skirt without knickers – for you and for any guy who happens to notice. You ever done that, gone out without your panties?'

I shook my head, and Lynn laughed.

'I don't mean wearing a miniskirt during a gale,' she said, 'although that can be fun. But you should try going out in a long skirt with nothing underneath, just for the experience. There's a strange sense of freedom, somehow. It's great feeling fresh air between your thighs, blowing up around your cunt, it really is. And it's almost like walking around half naked, but no one else knows.' She paused, thinking. 'I wonder what it's like being a nudist?'

'Everyone else would know about that,' I said.

'Yeah, but imagine being on a nudist beach. Seeing all those guys, all those cocks.'

'See one, seen 'em all,' I said – as if I knew all about the subject.

'Yeah, I know. It isn't even as though they'd be erect, is it? And what good is a limp dick?' Lynn suddenly turned her head towards the door, listening. 'Speaking of which, that's my little brother out of the bathroom at last. I'm going to wash my hair. You can try on anything you want, okay? Anything except my knickers.'

'Why? You planning on wearing some tonight?'

Lynn laughed and left the room, closing the door behind her. I wandered around, touching various different clothes. I wasn't totally convinced that I needed to change, but Lynn was the expert. She'd asked me to go out, and so I ought to follow her recommendation. I wished she'd stayed to advise me, because I hardly ever went shopping. One reason for this was that until recently I'd never earned any money of my own and so had nothing to spend; I went shopping when I had to, when I really needed something new to wear.

If Lynn had possessed only a few things, it would have been much simpler, but because she had such a variety it was hard to know even where to begin. The best way to choose was by starting at the top, I realised, with a new top. I peeled off my sweater, stripped down to my bra, and set to work on Lynn's clothes collection. I tried on all kinds of shirts and blouses, examining myself each time in the mirror. I liked a lot of what I wore, but whenever I searched for a skirt which would go with what I had on I kept finding a top that I liked better.

I piled everything I'd tried on to the corner of Lynn's bed. Was it true that she'd never fucked there? I could see why, because with all the clothes scattered over it there wasn't much room for anything except sleeping. She'd told so many stories of screwing in all kinds of amazing places that it seemed strange for her to claim that there was anywhere in town she hadn't been fucked.

In this case, however, I believed her. I'd never been fucked in my bed; I'd never been fucked anywhere. Tonight, however, if I was with Lynn, who knew what was going to happen . . .?

'That looks good,' she said, as she returned. 'It goes with your hair. The glossy black contrasts with the whiteness of the blouse. You've got great hair, you know, and I like the way it ripples over your bare shoulder. I wish mine was thick and wavy.'

Lynn's own hair was wrapped in a towel, but I couldn't believe she was serious. Hers was long and blonde and shiny, mine was black and boring. She had taken off her T-shirt, under which she was wearing a lacy black bra. It was the first time I'd seen so much of her, and I was even more envious. She was so slim, her breasts so well-proportioned.

I was wearing an off-the-shoulder white satin blouse, and Lynn was right: it did look good. I pushed my bra straps down, trying to hide them under the short frilled sleeves, but they slipped on to my upper arm.

'You need a strapless bra,' said Lynn.

She must have had one, but I didn't ask – and she didn't offer. Wearing another girl's bra wasn't quite as intimate as wearing her knickers . . . not quite.

I studied myself in the dressing table mirror. Lynn was behind me, also watching. I found it was odd having someone else in the mirror, because I was so used to seeing just my other self there. It was as if I was also seeing another Lynn.

'Or no bra,' she added. 'That's what guys really like: a nice pair of tits bouncing up and down. And you've got a nice pair. If you don't wear a bra, it saves them trying to figure out how to get it off. A bra is so simple to undo, isn't it? But it just goes to prove what we all know, that most guys have got no brains. You wouldn't believe the number of straps and fasteners I've had broken. Take my advice – if you've got to wear a bra, get one of these.'

I watched as her reflection reached between her breasts. Her hands twisted, pulled – and her bra came apart. Lynn was wearing one which opened at the front. She unhooked it for a moment, pulled it open an inch or two, then clipped it together again.

It was the first time I'd seen such a bra, and my eyes met hers in the mirror. 'Is it okay if I wear this blouse tonight?' I asked. 'You didn't want it?'

'No, you wear it. It looks better on you than on me.'

'Without a bra?' I said, studying myself.

'Without a bra,' Lynn said.

She was right, I realised. So I slipped off the blouse, then reached behind, unhooked my bra and let it fall. In the mirror, I saw Lynn staring in amazement at my bare tits.

'What's the matter?' I asked, turning to face her.

'Er . . . nothing.' She shook her head quickly, but kept looking at my breasts. 'Nothing at all. I just didn't . . .'

'Didn't what?' I gazed at my boobs, thinking there was something wrong with them.

'Didn't . . . didn't expect you to strip off like that. I'm not used to seeing half-naked girls. You're so . . . *daring*!'

I didn't think I'd done anything unusual. Because I was so used to undressing in front of the mirror when I was on my own, I'd thought nothing of peeling off when Lynn was present. Now I felt embarrassment, but I tried to act casual. It was no use quickly covering myself up, pulling the blouse back on.

But what did it really matter? Lynn had seen my bare boobs. So what?

I shrugged, and my boobs bounced up and down.

'Nice tits,' said Lynn, and she smiled. 'It's odd, I know, but I'd willingly strip off in front of a guy, in front of a hundred guys. Being totally naked wouldn't bother me, but it would seem so odd to let another girl see my tits.'

'Why?' I asked. 'You've got tits, I've got tits. We're the same.'

'But we're *not*. Guys always look at girls with admiration, don't they? But when we look at other girls, we do it critically, comparing ourselves with them. Guys don't think like that. Okay, they don't *think*. They react, or rather their cocks do.'

'I don't think you'd have anything to worry about,' I said. 'You look good to me, and I think all the guys appreciate you.'

'Of course they do!' Lynn laughed. As she did so, there was a knock on the door. 'Yeah?' she said.

The door opened, and a fair-haired guy stepped into the room.

'Lynn,' he said, 'have you . . . ?'

Then he saw me. He halted, never finishing what he had begun to say. His mouth hung open, and his eyes were wide. All he could do was stare at me, at my bare boobs.

'Yes?' asked Lynn.

'Hello,' I said to him.

His face became pinker and pinker, then he turned around and hurried out of the room.

'You're so cool,' Lynn said. 'You didn't even move, didn't even try to hide your tits. Peter was the one who was embarrassed, not you.'

'Your little brother?' I asked, although he didn't seem that little to me. Peter must have been about my own age.

'Yeah. Never goes out. Just watches TV, listens to his stereo. Never had a girlfriend. Doesn't know what his dick is really for.' She shook her head. 'You're probably the biggest thrill he's ever had, flashing your tits at him and saying "hello".'

I'd been so surprised that I had never even thought about trying to cover myself. It didn't bother me that Peter had seen my bare tits, although it gave me a strange sensation to think that he might have enjoyed seeing me – and it was a pleasant sensation.

'Isn't that what I was just saying?' said Lynn, nodding toward my boobs. 'A girl can turn a guy on just like that.' She snapped her fingers. 'And it's great, isn't it?' She smiled. 'Imagine being a stripper, with a hundred guys watching you. All you have to do is take off your clothes and you can produce a hundred erections.'

'I'm happy with one,' I said.

'One is never enough!' said Lynn.

I glanced towards the door, wondering if it could be true. Had my bare tits given Peter a hard-on? That gave me an even odder sensation. I looked back when I noticed Lynn's fingers on her bra clip.

'If you can do it, then I can,' she said – and she let her black bra fall, baring her breasts.

It was my turn to stare. Lynn's boobs were wonderful, just like the rest of her. I felt as though she was undressing for me, which was another odd sensation. It must have been how a guy felt when he watched a girl undress. My nipples suddenly hardened, and I turned away so that Lynn wouldn't see. I pretended I was examining myself in the mirror, checking my make-up. But she could see me in the mirror, because I could see her – and I watched as her nipples also dilated, becoming even pinker as they grew harder.

'Can't have all the guys admiring your tits,' she said. 'Not when they can admire mine, too. If you're going bra-less, then so am I. But I can go one better than that. I'll wear a see-through top!'

'Have you got one?' I asked, as I turned around.

We faced each other, each just clad in our denims.

'You name it,' said Lynn, 'I've got it. We ought to find you a skirt to go with that top. And I know just the thing . . . if I can find it.'

As she spoke, she undid the top of her jeans, pulled down the zip, and wriggled out of them. I couldn't keep my eyes off her breasts, the way they swayed from side to side as she moved. If I found her boobs so seductive, it was no wonder that guys were fascinated by them. Peter probably did have an instant erection when he saw me.

Or maybe it was me, I thought. Perhaps there was something wrong with me. A girl shouldn't be so attracted to another girl's body. Was I a lesbian without even knowing it? I wasn't too sure what a lesbian was. They preferred girls to guys, I knew that. But what about me? I'd never been out with a guy. Was that significant? And unlike all the girls at work, I didn't like shopping.

I felt very confused, and all the time I kept watching Lynn, thinking what a fantastic body she had, wondering what it would be like to touch her, to feel her boobs . . .

She stepped out of her jeans, and revealed a pair of lacy black briefs which matched her discarded bra. She looked so great, supple and slender, so feminine. I remained absolutely still, my eyes locked on her perfect body. I hoped she was going to take off her panties, stand there wearing just a towel – around her head.

I'd never seen another naked girl. Was her pubic hair as blonde as the rest of her?

Yet at the same time as hoping she would become totally nude, I also wished that she wouldn't reveal everything.

Then she turned away, walked towards the wardrobe, and I remembered to breathe again.

'Get your jeans off,' she told me.

'That's what they all say!'

Lynn laughed, her delicious boobs bouncing up and down. 'You can't try a skirt on like that.'

I glanced towards the bedroom door.

'Peter won't be back,' she told me.

'Pity,' I said. 'I was hoping he would be.'

Lynn laughed again. I peeled off my jeans. Lynn looked me up and down, nodded her approval, and then we started trying on different outfits.

We finally decided what we'd wear. Lynn found me a short black cotton skirt to contrast with the blouse, and a pair of black and white suede shoes which would go with both of them. She was as good as her word and chose a flimsy top for herself. It wasn't totally transparent, although translucent enough to show her nipples; but she produced a red velvet waistcoat to wear above it. Her red skirt was longer than mine, but slit high up the side; and her shoes were red leather, with stiletto heels.

For most of the time we were only clad in our knickers: hers were black and lacy, mine were simple white briefs. All the while, my nipples remained erect. I tried to convince myself that this was because I wasn't wearing anything, that I was cold. But that wasn't true. It was summer, I wasn't cold. The real reason my nipples were hard was because Lynn wasn't wearing anything, because I was fascinated by her almost naked body. But what was the reason her nipples stayed so firm . . .?'

'If you want my make-up,' she told me, 'just help yourself.'

Although we'd chosen what we would wear, we weren't wearing it yet. We were still clad only in our panties. Lynn finally unwrapped the towel from her head and started to comb her damp hair. I sat down at the dressing table, studying the impressive array of lipstick and eyeshadow, of powder and cream, of mascara and rouge. If Lynn didn't open a clothes shop, she could have done equally well selling make-up.

'And there's some jewellery in the top drawer,' she added.

I pulled open the drawer, discovering that she was equally well stocked with earrings and bracelets, necklaces and brooches. And lying to one side I noticed something else. Although I'd never seen one before, I immediately recognised what it was.

'You can't borrow that,' said Lynn, knowing what I was staring at. 'I like my home comforts.'

Her right arm reached past me, pushing her vibrator to the back of the drawer. As she leaned forward, her breasts rubbed across my back.

It was the first time we had touched. We both froze, but her flesh was anything but frozen. Her skin felt burning hot against mine, and I could feel the hardness of her nipples on my body.

'You smell nice,' she whispered.

We both remained absolutely still, her flesh against my flesh. Lynn was so close I could feel the heat of her breath against the back of my neck.

'It's only soap and water,' I breathed.

'It's more than that,' she replied, as she inhaled. 'Guys are so lucky, they get to smell us. But what do we have to put up with? Sweat, that's what.'

She remained directly behind me, her bare breasts pressed against my naked back. I looked in the mirror, my eyes meeting hers.

'I hate the smell of sweat,' Lynn continued, 'of stale sweat. It's as if they've never heard of washing. But I love fresh sweat, fresh male sweat. The sweat they get from fucking is like some exotic perfume. I love licking it from their bodies. The taste reminds me of spunk. I wonder what a girl's sweat tastes like?'

It wouldn't take much for her to find out. My whole body felt damp with perspiration, and all Lynn had to do was put her lips to my skin and she'd discover the taste. I hoped she would, yet simultaneously wished that she wouldn't.

Lynn leaned back, standing up behind me. We could have looked at each other in the mirror, but instead I gazed at her make-up on the dressing table, while she studied her own reflection.

'Men always get the best deal, I suppose,' she said. 'We're better looking, but we have to look at them. We wash, so we smell better. And our bodies aren't covered in hair. I don't like hairy guys, do you?'

I shook my head, because that seemed the correct response.

'They're too much like apes,' Lynn continued, 'too much like our ancestors. I don't like kissing guys with beards, getting hair in my mouth. But I suppose it's not much different from when they lick us out. They must get hairs between their teeth.'

As she spoke, her hand slid down her stomach, her fingertips slipping into the elastic of her panties. That was when my eyes met hers in the mirror. She smiled and drew her fingers out, adding:

'And girls look so much better naked than guys, with our genials modestly covered with hair.'

'Our what . . .?' I said.

'Genials. That's what I used to think they were called. I'd seen the word "genitals" written down, but I pronounced it wrong. That's why I prefer to say "cunt" and "cock", because there's no problem with the pronunciation.'

'You think girls look better naked than men?' I said.

'Yeah. You look much better than any guy. The only interesting part of a guy is his cock. Or his wallet. But cocks look so ugly when they're limp, don't they?'

'Do they?'

Lynn laughed. 'I suppose they're always hard when you're around!' She bent forward again, kissing my bare shoulder.

'I thought you said you weren't a lesbian,' I managed to say, despite my surprise.

'I'm not. Not yet! But maybe we shouldn't knock it until we've tried it . . . '

'What?' I leaned forward, out of reach.

'Only kidding,' said Lynn. 'Move up.'

She slid next to me on the stool. I tried not to touch her, but it was impossible. My right side pressed up against her left; thigh and hip, arm and shoulder. We sat side by side, staring at each other for a few seconds, until Lynn reached for her eyeliner.

'But I wonder what they *do*?' she added.

'Who?'

'Lesbians. Aren't you interested?'

'Not really.'

'I am. The worst thing about sex is men, and so the idea of sex without men sounds wonderful. But no men means no cocks, so I wonder what they do?'

I shrugged. 'Everything else,' I said.

'But what is everything else?'

I'd no idea, but I said: 'What's the first thing you do with a guy?'

'This,' answered Lynn.

'This?'

'We get undressed.'

She looked at me in the mirror, and I looked at her.

'I'm undressed enough,' I said. 'I'm not taking anything else off.'

'No, no, I don't mean that.'

'What do you mean?'

Lynn shrugged, and her boobs bounced. We both watched them jiggle up and down in the mirror. Then I shrugged, and my tits also bounced. We both laughed.

'Do you like having your nipples sucked?' Lynn asked.

'Is that an offer?' I asked, because I knew it wasn't.

'Of course you like it, and so do I. But what do guys get out of it?'

'Maybe it's because they haven't got tits. That's why they like touching them, sucking them.' Or so I'd heard . . .

'Could be,' said Lynn, and she cupped her breasts. 'Is that why we like touching and sucking cocks, because we don't have them?'

'Perhaps they taste nice,' I suggested, watching her mirror image holding her boobs.

'Cocks? Of course they do.'

'You know what I mean: tits.'

'Perhaps,' Lynn agreed.

Then she lowered her head, while simultaneously her palm lifted her right breast. Her tongue flickered out towards the nipple, and a moment later her lips engulfed the pink flesh.

I watched in total amazement as Lynn sucked her own boob. I sensed that she'd wanted to kiss my nipple but had instead licked her own – and I knew that she would have had no objection if I began to suckle on her left tit. My pulse was racing, my skin damp with sweat, but my mouth was dry and I nervously licked my lips.

Then Lynn raised her head and the moment was gone, much to my relief . . . and disappointment.

'Doesn't taste of anything,' she said.

'Not even strawberry?'

'Strawberry?' said Lynn, glancing down at herself.

That was what her nipples were like, I realised. Pink and dimpled, like ripe fruit.

'I prefer raspberry,' she said, as she looked at my nipples – which were slightly darker than hers, the areolae not so large.

She reached for one of her lipsticks, took off the cap, and twisted it upwards.

'I enjoy doing that,' she said, gazing at it. 'It's just like the head of a cock growing up out of the foreskin.'

Lynn then applied the tip of the lipstick to her left nipple. The right one was still wet with her saliva. She smiled at herself in the mirror as her left nipple became scarlet. When she put the lipstick back on the dressing table, I picked it up and glided it across my upper lip. The tip felt warm.

We looked at each other in the mirror for a few seconds.

'I think,' I said, 'we ought to go out.'

'I think,' Lynn said, 'you're right.'

So we got dressed and went out.

But we didn't get very far, only to the end of the street.

'Shit!'

'What's wrong?' I asked, turning to Lynn, who had suddenly halted and was looking down at her foot.

'My heel's broken,' she said. 'Have to go back.'

We returned to her house.

'If you've just got to change your shoes,' I said, as Lynn closed the front door, 'I'll wait here.'

'Different shoes,' she said, 'different outfit.' Then she smiled and made her way upstairs.

I sat on one of the bottom steps, wondering how long she would be. Everything was quiet. Lynn's parents were out, but from upstairs I heard familiar music. It was the theme to one of my favourite programmes, and I realised that Peter must have been watching it in his room. While I waited, I might as well watch television for a few minutes. I made my way upstairs, past Lynn's room, following the music. It was coming from the room at the end of the corridor. The door was open a few inches, so I pushed it a little wider.

The television was on, but Peter wasn't watching it. He thought Lynn and I had gone, that he was all alone. That was why he was standing in front of the mirror.

Naked.

Masturbating . . .

CHAPTER FIVE

I could see all of Peter's nude body, because his back was to me and his front was reflected in the full-length mirror on the wardrobe door. Oddly, the first thing I really noticed was that his pubic hairs were as blond as the rest of him.

Half in and half out of the room, I froze. I knew that I should leave, that I shouldn't be there, shouldn't be peeping. Yet I wanted to stay, wanted to watch. Peter hadn't noticed me, he was much too involved in what he was doing. His cock was hard and vertical, his right hand sliding up and down its length.

And I was fascinated.

I knew exactly what he was doing; I'd heard the other girls talk about it often enough. But this was the first time I'd seen anyone do it, the first time I'd seen a fully naked adult male, the first time I'd more than glimpsed an erection.

Hardly daring to breathe in case he should notice me, I kept absolutely still. My eyes were focused on his shaft, watching as his fist rhythmically slid from the base to the tip. His eyes were closed, but his mouth was open and he panted. His breathing gradually became faster, and his hand also increased speed. Meanwhile, my heartbeat had begun to race.

Then he suddenly stopped. I thought he must be about to ejaculate, and I continued to stare, hypnotised. I'd heard so much from the others about male orgasm, and for the first time I was about to witness it for myself.

Nothing happened – but that was when I noticed Peter's eyes were now open. If I could see him, I realised, he could see me. And he was staring at me in the mirror . . .

Neither of us moved, we just kept looking at each other. Time seemed to slow, and it was as if we gazed at one another for ages; but it could only have been for a matter of seconds.

When Peter had walked into Lynn's room and seen my bare breasts, I'd made no attempt to cover myself. Instead, he was the embarrassed one. What happened now was similar, except that our roles were reversed. I felt myself blush, and I opened my mouth to mutter an apology, but was able to say nothing. All I could do was shake my head and start to back away.

Peter didn't try to hide that part of his erection which was not covered by his hand. He did the opposite. He let his right hand fall. His jutting cock was fully exposed – and I became still again, no longer retreating, mesmerised by the new and thrilling sight of a hard penis.

Had Peter turned towards me, I would have immediately left the room because it would have seemed wrong to remain. But because it was the reflection of his prick which I could see, that was somehow different. We continued staring at each other, our eyes meeting in the mirror. Peter's face was expressionless. When he had entered Lynn's room and gazed at my bare boobs, I'd said 'Hello'. Whatever the circumstances, that was what I'd have said the first time I met him; it didn't matter to me that I was half naked.

Peter's mirror image mouthed the word: *Hello*.

And it evidently didn't bother him that he was totally naked, that his prick was erect. In fact, the opposite was the case. He was glad he was naked, glad he had a hard-on – and glad that I was watching him, because it was something he wanted to share with me. I suddenly understood all of this, becoming aware that it was because of me that Peter had an erection. Seeing my naked tits had aroused him, and he had probably been thinking of me while he was stroking his tool. Then he had opened his eyes and seen me, the object of his lust, watching what he was doing.

It must have appeared as if his fantasy had come true – or almost. He still hadn't moved. Maybe he was waiting for me to remove my top again, or perhaps even to strip off, to become as naked as he was.

The mirror was like a barrier between us, as though we were both in a different world. Seeing Peter's reflection was almost like watching him on a television screen. His *Hello* had been silent, as if the volume control were turned down. We were only a few yards apart, yet we were in different dimensions. Although we could see each other, there could be no contact between us.

The Peter I was watching wasn't alone in the mirror world, however, because my other self was with him. I could see her image standing in the doorway behind him, also observing what was happening.

Peter raised his right hand towards his mouth, and he spat into his palm. Then he lowered his hand to his cock, running his fingertips around the end of his knob. The purple dome glistened with spit. He ran his fingers lightly over his vertical prick for a few seconds, then wrapped his hand around the shaft again, and his fist began to slide up and down the length of his manhood.

He kept gazing at me while he wanked, and I knew he was doing it for me – and thinking of me. I was his inspiration, and I felt both pleased and excited. Although I remained totally still, as if not to break the spell, inside I was trembling. I could feel the blood race through my veins, my pulse seeming to increase to meet Peter's masturbatory pace. My skin was damp with sweat, even my crotch was moist. And I felt a strange sensation inside my core, as though I was beginning to burn up from deep within.

Peter's hand slid up and down, up and down, his cock flesh lubricated with saliva, drops of which ran down on to his testicles. Now his hips also started to rock up and down, up and down. His mouth was open, his breath coming faster and faster, but this time he kept his eyes open, and they were focused on me – while my own were focused on his magnificent maleness.

Then his hand stopped its frantic movement and his whole body became immobile. His hips were thrust forwards, while his palm tightly gripped the base of his prick.

Then it happened.

A sudden fountain erupted from the head of Peter's tool, the jet of white arcing through the air and splattering against the mirror.

I gasped in astonishment and delight as I witnessed my first ejaculation. This was *spunk*, I told myself. It was *semen*, it was *sperm*. I'd never seen this before, never really imagined what it would be like. And there was so much of it! So much *come* . . .

The first spectacular eruption was swiftly followed by another, and a second spray of spunk splashed on to the mirror. Then there was another shot, and another. Each successive creamy streak was of lesser strength, hitting the mirror lower down, until there were five or six different silvery trails slowly dribbling down the glass.

I stared at the mirror in utter amazement, my mind in a whirl and my whole body seeming to spin. I felt weak, as if I was the one who had been drained. My senses had been overloaded, and I'd no idea what to say or do.

That was when Peter smiled, let go of his cock, and started to turn round towards me.

That was also when I turned and quickly left the room.

I had a great night out. After the way the evening had begun, there was no way it could have been otherwise. Somehow everything seemed different now; I saw far more clearly, I knew what was really happening in the world around me instead of just having to guess.

Superficially, the club where Lynn took me was for dancing and for drinking. But already I was well aware of its true purpose. Its sole function was as a place where males could meet females, and the only reason that any of them wanted to meet was so that they could fuck.

With everyone's inhibitions reduced by alcohol, the dance floor became transformed into the scene of a primitive mating ritual. Dancing was nothing but sublimated sex, where potential partners could choose one another. Flirting and foreplay, kissing and caressing, all were carried out under the flashing lights of the disco beat. Bodies writhed as if already frenziedly fucking, shook and quivered as though reaching orgasm. If they could have screwed right there, in public, in front of everyone, many couples would have done so. Instead, they had to go outside to fuck, doing it up against the walls of the car park or in the relative comfort of the cars themselves.

Wherever I went, guys had always looked at me, had gazed at my tits. I knew it was because they fancied me, but for the first time I really understood *why*.

Now I looked them in the eye, returning their gaze; and I deliberately danced so that my bra-less boobs would bounce and jiggle.

I was the one who was in control, I had the power, because finally I *knew*. I knew the effect that my body could have, what the sight of my bare breasts had done to Peter, and I was aware that there was very little difference on the dance floor.

Even when clothed, my body could produce a certain physical reaction in a male, a reaction which he couldn't command – but which I could. The way I behaved, how I acted and responded, the way I danced, could give a guy an erection. For the first time I used all of my feminine skills, doing my best to conjure as many potential erections as I could. I imagined all the guys who were fantasising about me, who would think of my body when they left the club, who would remember the way my tits had bounced when they went home and masturbated . . .

There seemed to be so many guys that night, and it was my own fantasy that I was the focus of attraction. But none of them really mattered to me, because I was thinking of someone else. It was Peter, of course. Peter and his cock.

They all had cocks, although I had no real claim over them as yet. I gazed at their crotches, at the bulges in their pants, visualising what lay within, and I could easily have found out exactly what was there. Plenty of guys wanted to go outside with me, wanted to take me somewhere else. All of them must have wanted to, or so I dreamed, but not all of them asked. Those that did all got the same answer: no answer.

They bought me drinks, and they believed they were dancing with me. But I was dancing with myself, dancing alone with the music. I was in my own dimension, my own world where I was at the centre of so much attention.

'We're going now,' said Lynn, nodding to the guy she'd picked up – who probably thought he'd picked her up.

'Okay,' I said, as I kept dancing.

'What about you?'

'It's okay, you go.'

'You've got someone?'

'I've got everyone,' I replied, and I laughed.

'I think,' said Lynn, 'I should get you home.'

'Why? I'm okay. Really. You go. I'll be okay. Really.'

'I brought you here, I'll get you back.'

'It's okay. Really. It's okay.'

'It's not okay. Stop drinking, stop dancing, you're coming with me.'

'It's okay. I'll walk home. It's okay. Really.'

'You're not walking. You couldn't walk. And stop saying "okay".'

'Okay.'

She grabbed my arm and led me off the dance floor. I was fine until then, but as soon as I stopped dancing I began to feel dizzy. Lynn took me across to her new guy. For some reason I had trouble focusing on him, but it didn't really matter. He was just some dick in pants.

'She's coming with us,' Lynn told him.

He gazed at me, but it was a very different look from all the others I'd received from guys that night. 'Is she all right?' he asked.

'I'm okay,' I said. 'Let's have another drink.'

He shook his head. 'No,' he said to Lynn. 'I'm not having her being sick in my motor.'

'Yes,' Lynn said to him. 'Without her, you don't get me. You've just got to take her home, and then after that . . .' She smiled teasingly, then glanced around. 'But if you won't, I'm sure I can find someone else who'd be happy to give us a ride.'

The guy looked at me, looked at Lynn, looked at me again.

'There's two of us,' Lynn pointed out, 'me and her. We do a good double act.'

'She couldn't do anything in her state.'

'You'd be surprised what Sweet Lips can do.'

I glanced at Lynn. *Sweet Lips . . .?'*

Lynn winked at me, then started to lead me back towards the centre of the club again. 'If you're not interested,' she shrugged, 'I'll find someone else.'

'All right, all right,' he said. 'Let's go. My name's Michael.'

Lynn shrugged again. It wasn't his name she was interested in.

We followed Michael out into the car park. I felt so tired, and my limbs were very heavy. I must have been exhausted from dancing, blinded by the lights, deafened by the music. Without Lynn, I wouldn't have been able to move. The stars were spinning around and around high above me, streaks of brightness flashing across the midnight sky.

Lynn sat in the front next to Michael, and I sank down into the back seat. It was so wonderful to be able to sit down at last. There was even enough room to stretch out, so I did, and I closed my eyes for just a moment.

I wouldn't sleep, I knew; and I knew I couldn't sleep. My body might have been weary, but my mind was fully alert, thinking of all the strange new events that had happened over the last few hours.

Lynn was talking, but I wasn't really listening because my attention was concentrated elsewhere. In any case, what she said wasn't directed at me. She was narrating one of her sexy exploits, partly to keep Michael entertained while he drove, partly to let him know what a great time she could give him if she wished.

'She's my best friend, we share everything. Our clothes, our men. I tell her who I've been screwing, if he's any good or not, whether he knows how to use his cock properly. Recommendation is the best kind of advertising, and Sweet Lips will usually take my advice and try him out for herself.'

The name sounded vaguely familiar, then I remembered. Sweet Lips. It was what Lynn had called me. She was talking about me . . .

'And if she's had a really good shafting, Sweet Lips will always let me know – and then it's my turn to sample the guy, find out if his prick lives up to its reputation.'

I'd always suspected that Lynn made up much of what she said, and here was my confirmation. It wasn't that she was lying, not really, just that she was very inventive. Her horny tales were probably based on the truth, although she tended to exaggerate. I couldn't help wondering where the name Sweet Lips had come from.

'Have you got a friend?' Lynn asked.

'A friend?' said Michael, and it sounded like a word he didn't use very often. 'Yeah, I've got friends. Lots of friends. Why?'

'We could have a real party if there was another guy. Two guys, two girls, that's my kind of arithmetic.'

'Two girls, one guy,' he replied, 'that's my kind of arithmetic.'

'That can be fun,' Lynn agreed. 'But if you're a girl, it doesn't really add up. One guy equals one prick, so he can't really keep two girls happy at the same time. Believe me, there aren't that many guys who can simultaneously fuck and tongue twat. But one girl can easily keep two guys very happy. Or more than two guys. Sweet Lips is really great at that. Two guys, no problem. One cock in her cunt, another in her mouth. I've even seen her with two cocks in her mouth. Careful!'

I felt the car swerve, heard the sound of a horn, but none of that seemed important. I was thinking about what Lynn was saying, how I'd had two cocks in my mouth. But it wasn't me, I knew. It must have been my double, Sweet Lips, the girl in the mirror.

'Two in her mouth?' said Michael. 'Honest?'

'Honest,' Lynn told him. 'I've seen Sweet Lips do all kinds of things you've never even thought of.'

'You mean you've . . . you've watched?'

'Yeah. I've watched her, she's watched me. That's the great thing about a foursome, you can take a rest, be a voyeur, then join in again. I've watched Sweet Lips fuck, watched her suck, and she's watched me. You mean you've never screwed a girl while she was sucking someone else? Never watched a couple of girls fucking and sucking another guy, knowing it was your turn next?'

'Sure, sure,' Michael assured her, 'sure I have.'

'So that's why you don't want to do it again? You always want to do something new?'

'No, no. I can find a friend if you want.'

'It's up to you. We can keep it more intimate, just me and you. For a while. Then I can watch while it's Sweet Lips and you. I like watching. I'd like to watch her run her wet tongue all the way down your cock, licking your balls, drawing them into her mouth, then releasing them, working her way up your shaft again until she sucks and sucks your whole length between her sweet lips. She does it so well. Just watching her in action really turns me on, because I've felt how good she is with her tongue.'

'You mean . . . you and her . . . you . . . you do it . . . do it to each other?'

'Yeah. And if we hadn't met you, that's what we'd be doing right now. We'd already have torn our clothes off, and our lips would have been all over each other, tongues licking, lips sucking. Sweet Lips is just so . . . so sweet. When I say we're best friends, that's exactly what I mean.'

Best friends, that was a slight exaggeration, although it was nothing compared to the hyperbolic flight of fancy into which Lynn had launched herself. I pictured the two of us entwined together, my tongue exploring her nude body, while her lips ventured across my naked flesh. The idea fascinated and intrigued me, but it also made me smile.

This was more than a mere story, I knew. Like all her other erotic tales, Lynn must have based her narrative on fact. Was she really sexually attracted to me?

Probably – because I was attracted to her.

'You . . . you still could . . . still could do that,' said Michael.

'While you watch?' asked Lynn. He must have nodded because she laughed. 'That's great, because we like to be watched. Sweet Lips loves the taste of twat, adores swallowing sperm. Male or female, she can never get enough. She's insatiable. Absolutely cunt crazy. Totally cock crazy.'

As my concentration drifted away, I decided that Lynn was partly correct. Maybe I was cock crazy, because that was what I'd been thinking about for most of the evening. Only one cock had captured my attention, however, and it belonged to Lynn's brother. Even now I was still thinking of Peter and his penis, remembering how he'd masturbated for me.

And my memories dissolved into dreams . . .

Like everyone else, I suppose, my dreams are always weird and senseless, a bizarre mixture of fact and fantasy, conjured from events that had happened to me while awake and things which had almost happened, or might have happened – or that I wished had happened.

And so as I slumbered in the back of Michael's car, my dreams were of bare boobs and spurting spunk, or soft female flesh and hard virile cocks.

Lynn wasn't the only one who could devise wildly erotic episodes. My subconscious mind was every bit as inventive and dirty as her fertile imagination.

But when I drifted towards consciousness, I became aware that not everything which Lynn said was totally fictitious, that some of it was true. She did, for example, fuck inside cars.

Which was what she was doing now, on the front seat.

At first I believed I was still dreaming. Lynn wasn't really straddling Michael, wasn't really bouncing up and down on his lap, wasn't really moaning ecstatically.

But she was. She was turned towards me, facing me, and she smiled as I slowly sat up, stretched and leaned against the back seat.

'Oh,' she sighed, 'oh, oh, oh, oh . . .'

She put her hand to her mouth, miming a yawn, then blew me a kiss.

She was actually *fucking,* I realised, being

fucked. . .

From where I sat, there wasn't anything I could see, but I was aware that Michael's cock was sliding in and out of her cunt. Even so, Lynn didn't seem to care that I was there, so close I could have reached out and touched her. As with Peter when he noticed that I was watching him wank, it probably gave her an extra thrill to know she had an audience.

'Is that it?' she suddenly said.

I thought she was speaking to me, but she was talking to Michael. She had become still and was looking at him.

'Well . . . yes . . . for now,' said Peter.

'I'll walk you home,' said Lynn, and this time she was talking to me.

She clambered off Michael, climbed out of the car, opened the back door and held out her hand to me. When I got out, I noticed that we were around the corner from where I lived. It was a very quiet corner, and it was very late and very dark, or else the neighbours would have had a new scandal to gossip about for months and months.

'What about him?' I asked, as we walked away from the car.

'He's not going anywhere,' said Lynn. 'Not without me. Are you all right?'

'Yes.'

'Enjoy yourself tonight?'

'Yes.'

'I thought you did! And so did I. I'll see you at work on Monday.'

'Thanks, Lynn,' I said, and I squeezed her hand.

We looked at one another and both smiled. Lynn returned my squeeze, pulling on my hand as she did so, bringing me closer as she leaned forward to kiss me good night. Possibly she only intended to kiss my cheek, and possibly I turned my head towards her. In any case, her lips touched mine. It should have been for only a brief moment, the lightest of touches – but neither of us pulled away.

Her mouth was warm against mine, and I could feel her hot breath – and taste her sweet lips . . .

Perhaps it was my mouth which opened first, or maybe it was her lips which parted, but suddenly our tongues touched. There was a moment's hesitation and then they intertwined, advancing and retreating, from my mouth to Lynn's, back again, wetly embracing as we passionately kissed. Her arms hugged me tight, her inviting body rubbing against mine; my arms went around her, holding her even closer. I could feel the warm softness of her breasts squashed against my body, the hardness of her nipples seeming to tingle against my flesh.

As we kissed fiercely, intensely, tongues clashing, my eyes met hers – and I realised that Lynn was almost as drunk as I was.

Then we swiftly pulled away, releasing one another, and no longer could we look each other in the eye.

'Errr . . .!' said Lynn, as she glanced down.

'What?' I said, thinking how kissing her hadn't been that bad. It had been very pleasurable, in fact. But from Lynn's expression, she must have thought differently.

'Spunk running down my thigh,' she

explained, and she laughed briefly. 'See you later.' Then she spun round and walked away.

I watched her turn the corner, heard the slam of a car door, the growl of the engine followed by the sound of the vehicle driving away, and I looked up at the stars. They had stopped moving. I'd slept for a while, but now I was fully awake, I ran my tongue across my lips, remembering Lynn's kiss, and then I went inside and up to my room.

As I stripped off my clothes, or rather Lynn's clothes, and stood gazing at my naked image in the dressing table mirror, my mind relived the last few short hours. So much had happened.

I remembered removing my bra and how surprised Lynn had been when I revealed my bare boobs. Then she had done the same, exposing her wonderful breasts to my admiring gaze. But that was not enough, Lynn always had to go further. I knew now that it was no accident that she had rubbed her tits across my back; and then she had licked one of her nipples, decorating the other with a ring of lipstick.

I touched my fingertips to my mouth and leaned closer to the mirror; I could see where Lynn's shade of lipstick blended with my own. It had been quite a night.

But without a doubt the highlight of the evening had been Peter's performance, and I'd been thinking of him and his cock ever since.

I opened a bottle of baby oil, and as I started to remove my make-up I studied my reflection. My other self had also been there while Peter jerked off, watching from the background. I was so astonished that I'd simply stood there, a passive voyeur, but had something else happened in the mirror world? Had my image behaved differently?

Perhaps Sweet Lips had moved closer to Peter, had put her hand on top of his, joining in the rhythm of his strokes. Maybe her hand had even replaced his, her palm tightly gripping his prick. Possibly it was she who had tossed him off, her fingers wrapped around his tool when his spunk had spurted.

Peter had walked into Lynn's room when I was topless, but perhaps in the mirror world my other self had remained half clad when she watched him wank – or was even totally nude. Sweet Lips could have been as naked as Peter while she masturbated him, and instead of his semen splashing against the mirror it had cascaded across her nude body, hot drops speckling her bare boobs and dripping down her flesh towards the heart of her femininity . . .

Sweet Lips must have been remembering this, because I watched as she tilted the bottle of oil to her breasts, allowing the drops to splash on to her body. She cupped her tits in her palms, massaging the lubricious liquid into them, caressing her hard nipples with her thumbs. Her eyes were half closed as she enjoyed the sensation of stroking her own soft flesh.

A trickle of oil had escaped and slowly coursed its way down between her breasts, over her ribs, on to the flatness of her stomach. She traced its path with the tip of her index finger, never fast enough to catch it, and it oozed into the black curls of her pubic triangle – and her finger followed, down, down, down . . .

I kept looking, amazed at her daring, and watched as her index finger was joined by her middle finger. They paused in their descent, but they did not cease moving. Pressing hard, her fingertips started a circular movement, smearing the oil across her pubis.

Sweet Lips' lips parted with pleasure as she rubbed and rubbed at herself, and I heard her sigh with delight.

Then her fingers resumed their slow descent, still sliding from side to side as they slipped lower, deeper.

My heart raced, knowing where she was aiming.

Then she reached her target, the mirror exposing her most intimate flesh to my gaze, and I watched as she luxuriated in the sensuous attention of her expert fingertips.

She gasped with pleasure – and so did I.

Because there was only me, me and my reflection, and I looked away from the mirror and gazed down at the pink bud of my clitoris as I gently stroked it for the first time.

This was me, I realised. It was my body. It was my fingers which had begun exploring myself. It was my cunt that they had finally discovered.

And I moaned in total ecstasy as I achieved my first ever orgasm.

CHAPTER SIX

I had a great night's sleep, full of wonderful dreams, and it was late Sunday morning by the time I finally awoke. Normally I stayed in bed as long as possible whenever I had a day off work. I'd switch on the television, and maybe I'd read a magazine. That morning I did neither. I simply lay where I was and let my hands rove across my naked body.

When I touched my breasts, my nipples were already erect, and I stroked them with my palms, teased them between my fingertips. That was what I'd seen Sweet Lips do last night; but Sweet Lips was me, and that was what I'd done to myself. I'd also done a lot more, and my right hand slid down my bare flesh, following the route it had first explored last night.

And I discovered that it was also possible, and equally as pleasurable, to masturbate when lying in bed . . .

I was sober now, however, and not so uninhibited as I had been last night. Part of me wanted me to hold back, believing I shouldn't be doing this; but another part craved the tender caress of my fingers across my cunt. It was the latter urge which prevailed. For the second time ever, I found my clitoris and I gently rolled the sensitive bud of flesh between my fingertips, feeling it grow at my touch.

It took longer to come this time, because previously I'd worked myself up to fever pitch before touching my twat. Now I continued to stroke my breasts, my left hand moving from my left boob to the right, then back. The middle finger of my right hand stroked my clit, while the index finger and third finger slid across my vaginal lips.

I felt the tremor quickly building up deep within, and suddenly a shattering orgasm shook me from head to toe and left my whole body quivering with utter pleasure. I kept my hand across my trembling twat, fingers tight over my swollen labia, which were warm and moist from my flowing juices.

Kicking the covers away in the hope of becoming cooler, I gazed down at my nude body. My flesh was pink with exertion, damp with sweat. What I'd done now and the previous evening was not very much different from anything I had done previously. I'd stroked and touched myself before, but my fingers had always retreated before they became too intimate with the rest of my body. Last night I'd reached the threshold for the first time – and surpassed it.

Now I lay totally relaxed, both drained and yet also invigorated. I smiled contentedly, and I recalled how I'd once studied the dictionary, only to find there was no such word as *masterbate*. That was very confusing because it seemed like a medical term, and so it should have been included. It didn't sound like slang, such as *wanking* or *tossing* or *jerking off*. Then I'd noticed the correct spelling and found that *masturbation* was a noun; it meant *self-abuse* – and that confused me even more. What did *self-abuse* mean?

How could people abuse themselves? All I could think was that it meant doing something very unpleasant – like hitting yourself, hurting yourself. Self-abuse must have been self-torture, causing great pain. So why did anyone do it?

Now I knew. The true definition of masturbation, I had at last discovered, was the exact opposite. It was the antithesis of pain: it meant pleasure, total and absolute.

And I loved it. Why hadn't I abused myself like this before . . .?'

I obviously had a lot of catching up to do, but I intended to make up for lost time. Practice makes perfect. Reluctantly, I drew my hand away from my cunt and lazily stretched my whole body, rolled out of bed, and went for a bath – where I did some more practising.

As I walked back to my bedroom, I knew it wouldn't be too long until I was an expert. I'd spent twice as much time as normal in the bath, and I was very tempted to go straight back to bed and play with my new toy: my clitoris.

I'd deliberately avoided the dressing table mirror, but at last I stood in front of my image for the first time that morning. Sweet Lips was gazing back at me, also wrapped in a towel. Quick as a flash – literally – I pulled open the front of the towel. My reflection was equally as swift, baring her breasts and pubic triangle for me. I discarded my towel, and so did she. I rested my right leg on the top of the dressing table, checking the nail varnish on my toes, and my image did the same with her left leg.

As she did so, I caught a glimpse of pink at the junction of her thighs. She paused, becoming aware of my gaze, and she spread her legs even wider. For the first time I was able to see all of Sweet Lips' vulva: the reflection of my own labia and clitoris.

I suddenly wondered if this was what Lynn had meant when she'd used the words 'sweet lips'.

My left hand went to my mouth, remembering the way Lynn had kissed me. My right hand slid down, over my damp pubic curls, towards my vaginal lips. Last night I'd wondered if she fancied me – because I thought I fancied her; although I'd have fancied anyone who could kiss the way she had.

This was the first time today that I'd thought of Lynn and what had happened yesterday evening. Neither had I thought of Peter. Last night, it had been the memory of his jetting prick which had prompted me to explore my own body – just as I was convinced that his erection and ejaculation had been inspired by me. This morning, however, I'd had no need of any external stimulus. My mind had been focused on only one person, the one who I really fancied. Myself. And I was the one who had given myself such unbelievable pleasure.

But what had Lynn really meant by calling me Sweet Lips? Had it been just a story that she'd made up for Michael? Or was there more to it than that? Because then she'd kissed me, and I'd found out how sweet Lynn's own lips were. Or had she meant my genitals?

My *genials*, as she'd once believed they were called, and I smiled at the idea.

Last night, Lynn had wondered what it was that lesbians did, but she must have known because it didn't take me much to guess. They did everything that men did, with one exception. They kissed, mouth to mouth, lips to lips. Sweet lips. Mouth to vagina, kissing cunt . . .

I needed to see Lynn as soon as possible. Although I'd see her at work the following day, that wouldn't be the right place. So many amazing things had occurred since I arrived at her house last night that I felt I just had to talk to her.

It wasn't that I hoped or expected that anything was going to happen between us. Nothing physical. That moment had passed. But I wanted to let Lynn know about my phenomenal discovery, the discovery of myself, of my own inner sexuality. I didn't know how I'd express this, certainly not in words, and I wasn't going to describe how I'd stroked my cunt, even though I felt as if I'd invented it. Compared to Lynn, I was such a novice. She was the expert, and she even had a vibrator in her drawer. Knowing her, at the slightest excuse she'd probably have dropped her knickers and demonstrated her favourite technique.

Lynn had always pretended that she believed I was sexually experienced, although my innocence must have been very apparent. I somehow needed to communicate my new awareness with her – or with anyone. It was only a first small step for a girl, but it was a giant leap compared to my previous knowledge.

Today, my own cunt. Tomorrow . . .?

I stared at my mirror image, at the index finger which had slipped within the blackness of my damp curls and was slowly slithering lower, pressing harder. As I watched, I imagined the next stage of my sexual education.

It wouldn't be my finger which was exploring my cunt; the finger would belong to someone else – and someone male.

Later, that finger would be followed by something else which was definitely male. The most male thing that there could be.

I became slightly dizzy at the thought, imagining a cock sliding up into my cunt, wondering what it would be like to fuck for the first time, to make the ultimate transition from girl to woman.

Peter's tool had seemed so long, so thick. How could such a thing possibly fit into my twat?

And as I thought this, I watched the tip of Sweet Lips' index finger slide deeper between her legs. Then the end of her finger vanished, the first joint having curved up inside her vagina. I glanced down and saw that my own fingertip had also disappeared, buried up to the knuckle within my cunt.

Until now I'd only masturbated by caressing my clit and stroking my labia, but here was another fantastic sensation, a wonderful new experience which made me gasp with pleasure. Sweet Lips and I stared at each other's crotch as we finger-fucked ourselves for the first time.

After ringing the bell several times and getting no

reply, I'd already begun to walk away when I heard the door opening. I turned around. Peter was standing there, and we looked at each other for a few seconds.

'Hello,' I said, repeating the one word I'd ever said to him.

'Hello,' he echoed, which was the first time he'd spoken to me – although his naked reflection had mimed the same word.

His eyes changed the direction of their focus, staring at my boobs. I was wearing a white T-shirt, and I had no bra beneath. Neither did I have on any knickers . . .

I would have put on a pair of jeans, but my only good ones were still at Lynn's, so I'd dressed in a red cotton skirt. As I dressed, I'd remembered Lynn asking if I had ever gone out with no panties beneath my skirt. Having experienced so many new things recently, I thought I might as well try another one. And I had to admit that as I walked to Lynn's I did enjoy the sensation of fresh air blowing around my crotch – maybe because after all the internal heat it had generated I felt that my cunt needed cooling down.

Peter kept looking at my tits, so I looked at his crotch. When he noticed where my eyes were aimed, he half turned away; but then he smiled and leaned against the door frame, a posture which meant his groin was thrust towards me.

'You want to see Lynn?' he asked.

'Yes,' I said. 'I've brought back her things, the ones I borrowed.' I held up the bag containing her clothes, which provided my excuse for visiting.

Peter shook his head. 'There's no one here. She's out.' He paused, shook his head again.

'I don't think she's been back since last night.'

That seemed strange. She couldn't still be with Michael, could she? Lynn had told me how she hated spending the night with guys, that she preferred to return home to her own bed. But that was probably just another of her stories.

'I can give them to her,' said Peter, holding out his hand for the bag.

'There's some of my stuff in her room.'

'Okay, come in.'

I hesitated, thinking about the last time I'd seen Peter, not sure whether to go in or not.

Noticing my uncertainty, he said: 'I promise I won't take my clothes off.'

'Pity,' I said.

We both laughed. He stepped aside, and I went into the house. We glanced at each other, and I wondered if this was the real reason why I was here: had I come because, unknown to my conscious mind, I actually wanted to see Peter, not Lynn? My nipples became hard and my heart began to beat faster as I remembered watching his pulsing cock and how it had probably been the sight of my naked breasts which had prompted his erection and orgasm. I looked away, so that he couldn't read my thoughts through my eyes.

Because I wanted him to jerk off again – and I wanted to watch him again.

I tried to make the thought disappear. It was only by chance that I'd witnessed Peter wanking. Because it had happened once, that didn't mean it would occur again. Such moments couldn't be recreated. They couldn't be arranged; they had to be spontaneous.

What did Peter think of last night? He hadn't

been embarrassed then, and it didn't seem to bother him now. Was he also remembering what had happened? Did he have another erection?

I tried not to stare at his crotch, although I couldn't prevent another quick glance. But because of his thick denims, there was no way I could tell the state of his anatomy. Meanwhile, Peter was looking me up and down, from my sandals and bare legs up to my eyes, and we gazed at one another again.

'About last night,' I said, thinking that I had to say something. I ought to try to explain because I felt somehow guilty, and for all kinds of complex reasons none of which made logical sense. But then I became silent, wondering what there was I could say.

'Last night?' Peter frowned as if not understanding. 'Saturday, wasn't it?' He scratched his head, running his fingers through his almost white hair. 'Why? What happened?'

'I just want you to know that I wasn't spying because Lynn broke her heel which is why we had to come back and I was waiting for her downstairs when I heard your television so I thought I'd watch something until she got changed and your door was open and . . . and . . .'

Peter waited for me to continue.

'It was just chance,' I told him. I shrugged, which made my boobs bounce.

'I know,' he said, his eyes on my tits. 'It was the same when I went into Lynn's room and saw you half dressed. Chance.' Then he shrugged.

'Yes,' I agreed.

'But I turned around and walked away.'

'Er . . . yes . . .' Again I wondered what I could say, how I could justify not leaving as soon as I'd seen what he was doing. But why should I have to justify myself? It had been obvious that Peter wanted me to stay, wanted me to watch him masturbating. He knew this as well as I did, and so there was no reason for me to say anything more.

'Can I go up and get my things?' I asked, nodding towards the stairs.

'Yeah, go ahead.'

I hurried up the stairs, hoping that my skirt would bounce up as I ran – thinking that if Peter saw my bare behind we would be more even, that it would make up a little for my intrusion of last night.

And maybe I also hoped that the sight of my bare ass would provoke him again . . . although provoke him to do what, I wasn't sure.

'Anything you want?' he asked.

I stopped and quickly turned, trying to make my skirt swirl around so that he could glimpse my unclad crotch. He was gazing up and I wondered how much of me he had seen. Had he even been watching? He must have been.

I looked down at him and shook my head, not sure what he meant.

'Coffee? Tea?' he explained, answering my unspoken question.

I knew what he meant. He wanted me to stay.

'Coffee please. White, no sugar. Thanks.'

Or maybe he was just being polite. I continued up the stairs and went into Lynn's room, and I wondered what would be the best way to get Peter out of his jeans and to persuade him to reprise his performance of last night. Perhaps what had happened couldn't be repeated, not exactly. It was chance that I'd seen him wanking, but this time the random factor had to be eliminated.

If only I'd known how simple it could have been . . .

At the time, I still didn't realise that the majority of guys were exhibitionists. The way Peter had behaved last night should have been my first clue. The male species has one favourite possession. The ultimate phallic symbol is the phallus, and they are always glad of the opportunity to display it for the admiring gaze of the opposite sex. They'll drop their pants at any excuse.

All I needed to have said to Peter was 'Can I watch you toss yourself off again?' and his cock would instantly have been in his hand.

What I had to do, I decided, was recreate the events which had led to Peter jerking off. If I'd arrived wearing Lynn's clothes, I'd have had the excuse of undressing in order to put on my own things. I considered stripping off and waiting until Peter brought the coffee, then I could pretend that he'd surprised me while I was changing. After having seen him naked yesterday, it seemed only fair that he should also see me totally nude.

But what if he called me downstairs for the coffee? I couldn't go into the kitchen naked; that didn't seem a very subtle technique. Even if he saw me nude in Lynn's room, he might get the wrong idea. It would be evident that I'd shed my clothes for him, and he might assume it was an invitation to fuck. I didn't want that, or didn't think I wanted that – how could I tell?

In fact, I didn't know what I wanted. Now that Peter was out of sight, I was no longer even sure that I wanted to see him wank. Probably the best thing to do was get my clothes and leave.

Before I could do that, I sensed I was being watched. I spun round and saw Peter peering around the doorway. He must have crept silently up the stairs. And I knew exactly why.

'Hoping to see my tits again?' I said.

For a moment I thought that he was about to vanish downstairs, but instead he stepped into the room, bit his lower lip to stop himself smiling, and nodded his head.

'Would you like to?' I asked.

He hesitated, wondering what I was up to, then nodded again.

'I'll show you mine,' I told him, 'if you show me yours.'

He knew I didn't mean he should take off his T-shirt if I removed mine. He glanced down at his crotch, which was where I was also looking.

'We could do yesterday all over again,' I continued. 'You can look at my boobs and I can look while you . . .'

He stared at me in amazement. 'You mean . . .?' He made a fist of his right hand and slowly raised it up and down.

'That's right. You like wanking, I like watching. Sounds the perfect arrangement.'

'You're kidding.'

'I'm not.' And to prove I wasn't, I quickly peeled off my T-shirt.

Peter's eyes focused on my bare breasts, and I shrugged in order to make them bounce.

'Well?' I prompted. I slung my T-shirt over my

right shoulder, covering my right tit. 'Do I get dressed again, or do you get undressed?'

Peter gazed at my left boob, at the hard pink nipple, and he reached for his belt buckle. He unhooked the top of his jeans and pulled down the zip. His cock was already hard, because the top of his tool peeped out above the elastic of his underwear.

'That looks nice,' I said, not trying to hide my smile as I studied the end of his prick.

Peter gestured for me to follow him, then turned and headed along the corridor. I followed, more slowly, and by the time I reached his doorway he was totally naked. He was standing in the same position as last night, facing the mirror. His hands were on his hips, and I could see the reflection of his erect penis. My image was also caught by the mirror, except it was her left breast which was masked. I dropped my T-shirt on to a chair. Peter turned round to face me.

I gazed at his hard cock, and he stepped towards me. He raised his right hand, and I realised that he wanted to touch my boobs. I moved back automatically, shaking my head, and he halted.

Peter glanced down at his prick. 'She doesn't want you to get too close,' he said. He looked at me again. 'If that's what you want.' He took hold of his tool in his right palm. 'And if this is what you want' – he slid his hand up, then down – 'I'll make myself comfortable.' Then he stretched out on his bed, lying on his back and supporting his head in his left hand, while his right hand lazily slid up and down his length.

My heartbeat began to pick up speed as I

watched, and I stepped inside Peter's room for the first time, gradually moving nearer to the bed so that I could get a better view. I wanted to see Peter's cock more clearly, and I wanted to see how he manipulated it. When I was a yard away, I halted; I was close enough to see everything I needed.

'You work at the supermarket with Lynn, don't you?' he said, while he wanked. 'It looks as though it's a boring job. Do you like it there?'

'Shut up.'

'Can I talk about my dick? You're obviously fascinated by it, and I can't say I blame you. It's a very handsome specimen of male flesh, isn't it? If you want to touch it, be my guest.'

When I'd consulted a more modern dictionary, I discovered that masturbation meant 'manual stimulation of the genital organs to produce sexual pleasure', and that a person could do it to himself or to herself – or to others. I now knew what it was like to produce my own sexual pleasure, and I'd already seen Peter manually stimulate himself. The next stage was obviously for me to masturbate someone else. But for the moment I resisted the temptation.

I ignored what Peter was saying, instead concentrating my attention on what he was doing.

His penis lay across his stomach, and it was almost as if he was trying to stretch it up towards his navel. At first, I thought that he was gliding his fist over his knob, from the domed head, down to the base, then back again. Instead, his fingers gripped the same skin all the time, which had the effect of sliding the flesh of his penis over the shaft, the foreskin alternately rising to cover the glans, then being drawn back to expose it once more.

He licked the fingertips of his left hand, wiping them around the ridge of his glans to lubricate the skin which slipped back and forth over the purple flesh. Peter was watching me, and he must have been imagining that we were fucking. His hand was my cunt, his spit the juice from my twat.

'Girls do this, don't they?' he said. 'Do you? Do you wank yourself? I bet you do. Why don't you do it now? Why don't you finger yourself while I jerk off for you? Do it for me. Go on. Do it. Do it now.'

Imitating what Peter had done, I touched the fingers of my left hand to my mouth, licking them with my tongue. Then I moved my hand lower, but not as low as Peter had done. I rubbed my fingertips all around my right nipple, wetting the areola, spiralling inwards until the nipple itself was covered in shiny spit. My palm caressed my boob, smearing saliva all over my breast.

'That's it,' said Peter, 'that's it.' His hand rode up and down, matching the rhythm of my left hand.

My right hand slid down my hip, easing into the waistband of my skirt.

'Yes,' he said, 'yes . . . ' His hand moved faster, faster.

My fingers round the button which held my skirt, undid it, and my skirt fell . . .

I stood naked.

Peter stared at my nude body—

— and instantly ejaculated.

'Ah . . .!' he gasped. 'Ah, ah, ah . . .'

I watched as his spunk spurted, splattering his chest. Then there was another gush of come, jetting through the air from his cock, followed by another creamy streamer and yet another, all of them splashing on to his flesh.

'Ah,' I sighed, as I continued stroking my breast, while my other hand slid from my hip towards my crotch.

I heard a noise in the distance.

'No!' yelled Peter.

'What?' I said.

'The front door!' he said, leaping up. 'Quick! Get your clothes on!'

Once I realised what was happening, I pulled up my skirt, grabbed my T-shirt and slipped it back on. It only took a moment. I heard footsteps on the stairs. Peter was still trying to wipe away the streaks of sperm he had shot over himself, and to give him time to get dressed I stepped out of the room and closed the door. Then I saw Lynn at the end of the corridor, staring at me in surprise.

'I came to collect my clothes,' I explained, quickly. 'Hello.'

'Hello,' she replied. 'Your clothes? Oh yeah, from last night. They're in here, come and get them. Sorry I was out when you arrived. I hope Peter hasn't been a nuisance.'

I followed Lynn into her room, which was when she took a long slow look at me.

And she knew, somehow she knew.

'*Peter?*' she said, and she turned her head as if she could see through the wall to her brother's room. 'Well, I suppose he does need educating.'

He wasn't the only one, I thought; but so far I

was the one who had done all the learning.

She was staring at where the saliva from my right boob had soaked through my T-shirt. She must have thought it was something else, because she said: 'What you do is up to you, of course. Just be careful. And make sure you don't get spunk on my clothes.' She shook her head in bewilderment. '*Peter*?' she said again, then she laughed.

'What about you?' I asked, trying to change the subject. 'Have you been with that guy all the time? What was his name?'

'Michael.'

'What happened?'

'Nothing much,' she replied, and she shrugged.

I'd expected her to narrate another inventively athletic sexual encounter. She didn't, which should have surprised me, but instead my mind was elsewhere; I was wondering what might have happened if Lynn hadn't suddenly arrived.

Peter had masturbated for me. Would I have done the same for him?

Despite the erotic heights to which I'd ascended, I doubted that I would really have finger-fucked myself while under the gaze of a voyeur. Peter might have been an exhibitionist, but I hoped that I wasn't.

It didn't seem very ladylike.

CHAPTER SEVEN

I kept visiting Lynn, and she would let me try on her clothes and wear whatever I wanted if she didn't need it. But we never took our relationship further than that first night.

If she ever discovered what it was like to suck another girl's nipple, it wasn't through tasting my tit. Neither did she rub her boobs over my bare flesh again, and we didn't even kiss – or at least not in the heat of passion, mouth to mouth, tongue to tongue, as we had that one memorable time.

We went out together occasionally, but not very often. Whenever I did go to Lynn's house, she would usually be out. That was because I timed my visits so there was no one in except Peter.

Peter and his cock . . .

His was the first penis I had ever encountered, and so it was only natural that I was fascinated by it. And I was also amazed by my power over his dick: the way that I could make it erect, cause it to ejaculate.

On Saturday evening, exactly a week after I'd first been to Lynn's, I rang the bell. I had to ring several times before Peter finally opened the door.

'Oh . . . it's you,' he said, as he studied his feet.

'It's me,' I agreed.

'Lynn's gone out.'

'I know, but I came to see you.' I'd already decided that there was no need for subtlety, not any more. 'I thought you might like to give me another demonstration.'

He met my gaze for the first time, and he tried not to smile. 'What kind of demonstration?'

'Peter and his performing penis,' I said, using a line I'd been rehearsing all week.

He was unable to prevent himself smiling, and he let me into the house.

'I can't just do it,' he said. 'Not to order.'

'Yes, you can.'

'I've got to be in the right mood.'

From what I knew, I very much doubted that. All a guy needed was an erection, which wasn't too difficult to arrange.

'I'm sure I can get you in the right mood,' I replied, and I touched my right breast with my left hand, simulating what I'd done six days ago.

Peter watched, remembering. 'But what do I get out of it?'

I stared at him, not understanding what he meant.

'I can wank on my own,' he said. 'I can do it any time. I don't need you watching me.'

Then I realized what he meant: he wanted to go further, to do something different.

'What you get out of it is an orgasm,' I told him. 'And how many times have you had that *and* a naked girl?' I shrugged and reached towards the door. 'But if you don't want to . . .'

'No, no,' he said quickly, and his hand pulled

mine back.

It was the first time we had touched, as we both realised. We stared at each other, his hand still on top of mine.

'Warm hand,' I said.

Peter curled his fingers around mine until my hand was almost a fist. 'Want to feel how warm my cock is?'

'No,' I said.

He laughed, let got of me, and started upstairs. 'The show's this way,' he told me – and I followed.

When we reached his bedroom, he waited for me to make the first move. This was what had occurred on both previous occasions; the first thing that happened was that he'd seen my bare breasts. This time I was wearing a checked shirt and a pair of jeans, and I also had underwear on.

'Let's have some music,' I said.

'What? Why?'

I didn't answer, instead walking across to Peter's stereo, where I checked through his cassettes and put one into the player. If he wanted something different, then I'd give him something different. The music started to play – and I started a striptease.

I danced with the rhythm, twirling around as I began to unfasten the buttons down the front of my shirt. I started at the neck, but only undid the first two, then worked my way up from the hem, tugging the shirt open wider and wider as each button came undone, exposing more and more of my bare flesh to Peter.

'More,' he yelled, 'more! Less, I mean! Less, less!' He was sitting on his bed, clapping his hands and cheering.

Then there was only one button holding the front of my shirt, and I held my right hand over it, also covering my bra. As I undid the last button, I quickly spun round, turning my back on Peter. I eased the shirt off my shoulders and pushed down my bra straps, so it appeared that I had nothing on underneath. Glancing down at Peter, I noticed he had begun to unfasten his own shirt.

In one quick movement, I had my shirt off and I threw it at Peter. It covered his head, and he brushed it aside, anxious to see my bare tits. Then he noticed I was wearing a bra, and he looked disappointed for a moment. Then he smiled, enjoying the way I'd fooled him.

The bra was brand new; I'd bought it a few hours earlier. Lacy and front-fastening, it was very similar to the one Lynn had worn. Except for the colour: it was nipple-pink. Although the colour blended in with the fabric, by now my nipples were prominently displayed through the thin material.

I'd resumed dancing, and I kicked my sandals towards Peter. He caught them both as I went to work on my jeans. There didn't seem to be any erotic way for me to peel off my denims, although for Peter it must have been very erotic simply to watch me remove them. I played with the zip for a while, gradually pulling it down as if I was about to drop my jeans, then drawing it back up again.

Then I let go of the zip and swung my hips from side to side, rocking my pelvis backwards and forwards, and my denims slowly slid down my bare legs. I stepped out of them and was left in just my bra and lacy pink briefs. Brief was the word, because there was a fringe of black hairs curling above the elastic.

By now Peter also had his jeans off – and he also had something sticking out above the elastic of his underwear.

I was dancing again, my hands caressing my body, rubbing my hips and breasts, stroking my torso and sliding down towards my crotch, then retreating at the last moment or else gliding down the inside of my thighs. Although I was facing Peter most of the time, watching his erection, I kept glancing at the wardrobe mirror. My image was also dancing, also stripping.

My hands moved upwards, stroking my boobs for a while until I crossed my arms, left hand to right breast, right to left, and my fingertips undid the hook in the centre of my bra. I pulled the bra open slightly, closed it again, then opened it slightly more, and kept on repeating the process until I almost exposed my nipples to Peter's appreciative gaze. Then I alternated each half of my bra, again almost revealing each nipple. Finally, I let the garment fall away completely, swiftly spinning around, so all that Peter saw was a brief glimpse of my left nipple.

Clad in only my pink panties, my back towards him, I continued dancing. From the way I shook my shoulders, he must have been aware how much my boobs were bouncing and swaying, but he was unable to see them. I was about to turn around, to let him watch my unfettered tits jiggling, when suddenly he was behind me.

He was completely naked, trying to dance. He wasn't very good at it, maybe because he was more interested in trying to touch me, to rub his hard cock up against my bare flesh. I managed to avoid his swinging knob, and to prolong the tease I kept my back to him. Whenever he attempted to go around me, I turned the other way. But when I danced between him and the mirror, he was able to see the reflection of my bare breasts bouncing.

That was when I began stroking my boobs again, fingering them with my left hand, covering each one in turn and then allowing the nipple to peep out from between my fingers. Meanwhile, my right hand roved across the rest of my nude body. This time I didn't avoid my crotch, at first my palm lightly gliding over the pink fabric, then lingering longer, pressing more firmly.

Peter had become still, having given up trying to stroke his knob against my buttocks, and his eyes were fixed upon my reflection. I met his gaze, and then my attention became focused on his vertical penis. How long before he took hold of his aroused manhood and began to wank?

As I thought of masturbation, my fingers slipped inside the elastic of my panties and ventured down. I kept on dancing, although my very core was absolutely still. It was as if all of my body was in rhythmic movement except my cunt, which remained steady in the firmament of motion, awaiting the probing touch of my fingers. My palm covered my pubis – and my other hand peeled off my knickers.

Then I spun around to face Peter, only my fingers hiding my cunt. He took a step towards me, and I threw my pink panties on to his bed; that was where I wanted him, and he understood. He halted and backed away, lying down on his side, his erection towards me.

Turning around once again, I gazed at my naked image. Sweet Lips and I removed our hands from our twats, and we smiled at each other. I pulled at the wardrobe door, checking the angle and wedging it open, before slowly walking across to where Peter and his cock lay waiting for me.

He hadn't yet begun to stroke his prick, and it was obvious that he wanted me to touch him. If he'd asked me to, I'd have refused. He must have realised I wouldn't take orders from him, because he said nothing.

I'd already done more than enough for Peter. But what I did next was for me, not for him.

I reached out and touched his knob for the first time, letting the index finger of my right hand rest on the firm flesh just beneath the swollen head. Then I lightly stroked my fingertip down one side of his maleness, through his white pubic hairs, and I traced the outline of his balls before bringing my finger back up on the opposite side of his shaft until it had ascended to the very apex.

Peter smiled, and so did I. Kneeling on the floor by the side of the bed, as near to his dick as I could be, I watched as my mirror image drew her finger away for a moment – then replaced it with her whole hand.

My fingers wrapped themselves around Peter's cock, absorbing the warmth of his skin, sensing the potency of his latent manhood, feeling the pulse as his blood throbbed through his swollen flesh. I felt his virility surge up my arm, radiating through my body and then spiralling towards my vagina, and my whole being trembled in anticipation.

I gazed in awe at what I possessed: at the thick

length of male flesh in my grip, from the domed head down to the heavy globes of his testicles.

'Now what?' I said, and I realised that I was speaking to Peter's knob.

It was as if it was something separate, that it had nothing to do with the rest of him. Then his cock moved, sliding up between my fingers, the foreskin drawing completely back, the ridge at the base of the glans becoming visible. His prick appeared to have a life of its own, and I quickly let go.

Peter laughed, and he drew his hips back. He had thrust himself forward, that was how his cock had appeared to move.

'Take hold of it again,' he told me, and I obeyed. 'Not too loose. Not too tight. That's good. So good. Just slide your fingers up. That's right. So good. Yes. Down. Nice and slow. That's right. Back up. Yes. Yes. So good. So very good. Down again. That's right. That's good. Easy, isn't it? And so nice . . .'

I did exactly as I was instructed, and I could see that Sweet Lips was doing the same. It made it so much easier knowing that she was with me, that we were both making this breakthrough together. My heartbeat was racing, and my hand began to pick up speed.

'Slow down, slow down,' Peter warned.

'Why?'

'Because it's nicer when it's slow, and it hurts a bit if you go too fast. You want to kiss it better?'

My hand became still.

'It needs some spit,' he said, 'that's what I mean. So it slides nice and smooth.'

I let go, lifted my hand to my mouth, and I

could smell his cock on my skin. My hand froze, and I inhaled the unfamiliar male odour, then allowed a trickle of saliva to drip on to my fingers. My fingertips returned to his dick, rolling around his smooth glans and coating it with spit. By now he was on his back, and I leaned over him, letting another dribble of spit flow from my lips along the length of his knob.

'So good,' he breathed, as I massaged my saliva across his shaft, from the dome down to his testes.

Touching his scrotum, I felt his balls draw up, tightening. I ran my fingertips back to the tip of his cock, where there was a bead of saliva. When I drew my index finger away from the glans, a fine thread of silk was stuck to it, like the web of a spider. This must have been spunk, I realised, a drop of which had oozed from the slit at the end of Peter's dick. I rubbed my thumb and forefinger together, examining the strange substance.

'Plenty more where that came from,' said Peter, as he took told of my hand and wrapped it around his cock.

He kept his hand on top of mine, guiding it up and down his shaft, up and down, up and down, until he thought I'd got the idea. Then he let go, and my hand continued its rhythmic stroking.

'So good,' he whispered. 'So good.'

My fingers rode his cock, and Peter's hips began to rock up and down, sliding himself between my palm. I could feel the blood rush through my fingers, and I wasn't sure whether it was my own pulse or the surge which flowed through his prick.

Then Peter became totally still, his whole body

tense, and his hand came down on mine again, holding it motionless. This time there was no doubt that the vibration I felt in my damp palm was coming from his tumescent tool. And deep within myself I could feel another tremor beginning to develop.

'Ahhh . . .!' gasped Peter.

His cock throbbed within my grip, spat, and the first spurt of spunk sprayed on to his chest, followed by another gush of come, then another, another.

I gazed in awe, in amazement, in admiration, at the drops of semen which lay across Peter's flesh, realising that I had created them. Far inside, I felt warm and wet. It wasn't an orgasm, not quite. The feeling was similar, although much less intense – but still very pleasant.

My right hand kept hold of Peter's prick, as though not wanting to lose it. There was no way I could retain his erection, however, because already I could feel the hard flesh start to soften. I watched as a final drop of spunk began to drip from the tip of his knob, catching it on the end of my thumb and wiping it across the glans. The rich purple of the head was beginning to fade as the glans retreated within the foreskin.

I reached over with my left hand, tentatively touching the streaks of spunk on Peter's chest. The creamy liquid was warm and smooth, and I ran my fingers through it, tracing patterns across his ribcage. When I raised my hand, my fingertips were smeared with his seed. I rubbed my fingers together, studying the unfamiliar texture, then lifted them towards my face, towards my nose, sniffing the strange scent.

Peter had laughed as I smeared come over his chest, but now he watched in silence as I slowly opened my mouth and tentatively thrust out my tongue. Then I had to laugh, and I drew my hand away.

'Think I was going to suck your spunk, did you?' I asked, as I gently squeezed my right hand, which still enfolded his wilting knob.

He shrugged and smiled, watching as I examined my fingertips again.

'As if I would,' I said – and I caressed my right breast, circling the nipple with semen.

I felt Peter's cock start to harden once more.

'How soon before you can come again?' I asked.

I often visited Peter, but I tried not to establish a regular routine. Although I enjoyed what we did together – I wouldn't have done it otherwise – I didn't want him to take me for granted, to believe that the only reason for my existence was to jerk him off.

Of course he wanted to go further than that, and each time we did go a little bit further, doing something different. But Peter wanted the ultimate. He wanted to fuck me, and I kept putting him off. I knew it would happen some time; I wasn't going to remain a virgin.

Because my first fuck would be an important part of my life, I wanted it to be special. However, I had no great romantic dream that I'd fall in love with my ideal hero, a man who would both bed me and wed me, someone with whom I could live in an orgasmic paradise forever.

But the way things were going, it seemed

almost inevitable that Peter would be the first guy to screw me. That wouldn't have been so bad, because I certainly knew him better than anyone else. We'd be lying on his bed one day and it would probably just *happen*. He'd be above me, but instead of rubbing the end of his knob across my pubic hairs to make himself come, his cock would slide into my cunt for the first time – and once it was in, we might as well fuck. It was the logical next step in our relationship, yet somehow it wouldn't be enough. I wanted some kind of *magic*.

Okay, so maybe I did have a great romantic dream . . .

Peter was fun to be with, good company. I learned a lot from him, about cocks and also about myself. We went out together as well as stayed in together. We even kissed.

I lost count of the number of orgasms I gave him, and they gave me almost as much fun as Peter. Right from the beginning, when all I did was show him my tits, I enjoyed giving him pleasure. If he liked being aroused and stimulated by my naked body, then that was enough reward. And when he ejaculated over my breasts, that was his offering to me. One reason I enjoyed rubbing his come over my flesh was that Peter liked watching me caress myself.

As well as watching me, he liked touching. At first, I did all the touching, stroking his cock and wanking him. Then I'd allowed Peter to touch my body, and I found that I enjoyed the attention of his hands and mouth. He adored stroking my breasts, licking the nipples, sucking them between his lips – and that was also my favourite place for him to kiss.

There might have been a different favourite except that one area of my body was totally taboo: my cunt. That was mine, mine alone. I'd only recently discovered my twat and still hadn't explored it enough for myself.

He could run his fingers through my pubic hairs, even tease them with his teeth. I didn't mind when he rubbed the end of his knob all over my pubis and his come turned my curls from black to white. But I never allowed him to so much as glide a fingertip between my thighs.

Even so, I felt jealous of how Peter could get so much closer to my cunt than I could. It was mine, but he could have seen my most intimate flesh in more detailed close-up, could even have touched my vulva with his tongue. If I'd permitted it . . .

The first time he'd blown his hot breath towards my cunt, my reaction was to clamp my legs together. Even though my whole body trembled with pleasure, I didn't want him to see how he'd caused my vaginal lips to swell and my clitoris to dilate.

When he'd begun to slide his wet tongue down towards the valley of my twat, I had remained similarly impregnable, although the drops of warm spit which had trickled so deliciously over my tender labia almost melted my resolve. It must have felt very much like spunk, I imagined.

Peter was as fascinated by my cunt, I realised, as I had been by his prick – or any prick. In fact, he was even more interested in my twat than I was in his tool. He kept wanting to thrust his tongue between my labia, to taste my clitoris, whereas I had no interest in sucking his cock and swallowing his spunk, even though he kept offering his knob to my lips as though it were some gourmet delicacy.

Although I licked and sucked Peter's nipples, it never seemed to thrill him as much as when he did the same to mine. It was obvious that he wanted more; but whatever I did, however lasciviously I behaved, he always wanted more.

Ever since my tits had developed, I'd had to get used to guys staring at them. Old guys, young guys, almost every male of the species was interested in boobs. But bare breasts had become public property, used in advertising, printed in newspapers, shown in films and on television, and girls thought nothing of sunbathing topless. There was no longer any great mystery about female breasts. In my own case, it seemed no big deal to bare my tits.

Instead, the centre of masculine attention had become the cunt – or so I learned from the glossy magazines which Peter kept under his mattress. I only knew they were there because I'd 'accidentally' seen them. He must have left them in view hoping I would become so passionately inflamed by their salacious contents that I'd immediately open my legs and let his prick slide deep into my eager twat.

I'd seen such magazines on sale, and I knew they contained pictures of naked girls, but I'd never imagined that they would be so amazingly explicit. Almost every girl in every issue had her legs spread, spread wide, and the focus in nearly every photograph was her shiny cunt. I could hardly believe the contortions of some of the models, the acrobatic poses they adopted in order to display their vulvas to the camera. In some of the photos the girls were redundant, without faces or bodies. Instead there were two-page spreads of enormous pink twats, of swollen vaginal lips and glistening clits in magnified detail.

Peter may have viewed an infinite number of glossy magazine cunts, but knowing how much he wanted to see the real thing, to study my labia and clitoris made me even more determined to keep my twat as much of an enigma as possible. It was too personal, too intimate; it was my secret, to be shared with no one.

This had nothing to do with fucking, or very little. He could have screwed me and, except for discovering that it was an exact fit for his thrusting knob, still known absolutely zero about my cunt. I suspected this at the time, it was one of the things the girls at work said which seemed totally credible, and my suspicions were later confirmed when I became more sexually active and experienced.

I've often thought that the expression 'he knew it like the back of his hand' would be more accurate if it was changed to 'he knew it like his own cock' – because that is every man's favourite possession. But when it comes to the female sexual organs, that's an entirely different matter. Because it's far more complex than their own genitalia, most men are as familiar with the vagina as they are with the dark side of the moon.

This is as much the fault of women as it is of men, and I know because of how I behaved with Peter. I refused to *tell* him and refused to *show* him. Men are too blatant, women too subtle. We are almost like two different species. We expect the other sex to instinctively *know* what to do to us, but that is never enough. We can be absolutely intimate together – naked, fucking – but we still can't *communicate*.

Peter wanted to see my cunt, but he never asked.

And when he asked to watch me masturbate, I refused.

His problem, my problem; my fault, his fault. Guilt and blame, blame and guilt. We could talk, but we never said anything. Maybe that was one reason why I didn't want to fuck Peter, because I wanted to connect with him on a more than physical level – and that was probably asking too much.

He hadn't seen my cunt, fingered my cunt, tongued my cunt. He had never brought me to orgasm, and I had never sucked his knob or even shown him how I gave myself a climax. In fact, when I considered our relationship, there were more things that we hadn't done than I realised.

But there was still something I could do for myself, that I wanted to do for myself, and whenever I returned from seeing Peter I'd bring myself to orgasm. Having been with him wasn't necessary, of course. I could finger myself to a climax even if I hadn't already stroked his knob until it produced its creamy fountain of man juice.

I continued to perfect my own masturbatory techniques, fingering my clit as I lay in bed, rubbing my inner labia while I was in the bath, spraying needle sharp jets of water all across my vulva when I was in the shower, sliding a finger or two deep into my cunt as I watched my reflection do exactly the same in the mirror.

Sometimes I'd bring myself off quickly, urgently, as if my very life depended on this personal race towards ultimate satisfaction, the fingers of both hands clutching my cunt, each fighting for possession of my clitoris. Other times I would treat myself more luxuriously, slowly climbing towards the peak, needing only one finger to guide the way, abruptly pausing, delightfully teasing myself, holding off as long as I could until my clit craved my touch, then I'd resume my ascent until I achieved yet another shatteringly sensational, shudderingly sensual, shiveringly splendid climax.

A girl's best friend is her cunt.

Sweet Lips and I shared a lot of fun together – and a lot of wonderful orgasms.

CHAPTER EIGHT

Peter opened the door to let me in, then headed straight for the stairs.

'You don't even say *hello*?' I said, without moving.

He paused, turned and looked at me. 'Hello,' he said. 'How are you? Nice weather, isn't it? Please come in. Shall we go up to my room and you can stroke my knob?'

By now it was all very routine, I realised, and for Peter I was becoming a habit.

'What about that cup of coffee?' I asked.

'What cup of coffee?'

'The first time you let me in, you offered me a cup of coffee. Remember? I'm still waiting.'

Peter had given me plenty of spunk, but no coffee.

'Okay,' he said. 'Go upstairs, strip off, and I'll bring you some coffee.'

'No,' I told him, as I entered the house. 'We'll keep our clothes on and we'll drink our coffee.'

'Okay, okay.' He shrugged and started along the hall, then he halted and looked back at me. 'This way,' he said, bowing low, and he waited until I walked past him. He followed me into the kitchen. 'There's the kettle, there's the coffee.'

I sat down at the table. 'White, no sugar,' I told him.

He stared at me for a few seconds, then filled the kettle, switched it on, and sat down on the other side of the table.

'Talk to me,' I said.

He shrugged. 'About what?'

'We never talk, do we?'

'We're usually too busy.' He smiled. When I didn't respond, he asked: 'Is something wrong?'

It was my turn to shrug.

I could almost see Peter's brain ticking over, wondering what we could talk about. Then he had an idea, and he mentioned a television programme he'd seen last night. Watching TV was still almost my favourite activity. Being with Peter, however, wasn't necessarily the first; I could still have more fun on my own.

'I preferred the first series,' I answered. 'It seems very repetitious now. Some of the best people have left. There are new characters, but they seem to be stuck with the same old plots.'

'I like that new girl, the blonde with the big boobs.'

'You would. She's only there to boost the ratings.'

'She boosts mine!'

'But she's just a cliché, isn't she? Blonde, so they make her a bit dumb. She's got the body, but not the brains.' I stared at Peter. 'A bit like you, I suppose.'

'The story of my life. Girls only want me for my body.'

He was being optimistic by using the plural – girls. I was sure that I was the only girl he was seeing. Lynn had once said that Peter had never had a girlfriend and didn't know what his dick was for. Soon after, however, I discovered that she wasn't totally correct about the latter. I'd learned a lot from Peter, but he'd probably learned even more from me.

'One part of your body,' I told him.

Peter laughed. 'What else is there?'

'I wish I knew,' I said, and I tried to think of an answer.

He didn't really have anything else to offer me except his knob; but that was what every man had. Sometimes I thought we'd done enough together, that I no longer needed Peter, it was time to move on. He didn't have any other girls, but neither did I have any other guys. If all I wanted was cock, then half the rest of the world was waiting for me.

Other times I would think that we ought to move on together. Peter was still a virgin, and so was I. We could easily rectify this situation. It was what he wanted, so why was I hesitating? Wasn't it better to accept a prick that I knew? Or would my first fuck be more memorable if I was introduced to the art of screwing by an expert? After all, you didn't take driving lessons from someone who couldn't drive.

Peter stood up and went over to make the coffee. There was a jar of roasted beans on the shelf, but instead he opened the instant coffee and spooned the powder into two mugs, poured on the boiling water, then turned towards the refrigerator for the milk.

I gazed at his crotch, thinking of the potent flesh which lay latent within the denim.

Something occurred to me and, as he opened the fridge door, I stood up and walked towards him. He took out the milk, and I knelt down in front of him and started to unbuckle his belt.

'Hey!' he said, although naturally he made no attempt to resist. 'What are you doing?'

But he knew exactly what I was doing, and there was no need for me to reply. As quickly as I could, I unfastened the belt, unzipped his jeans, tugged them down, pulled at his underwear – and gazed at his limp dick. Until now, Peter's prick was always rigid by the time his pants were off.

'Whenever I see you,' I told him, and it was as if I was talking to his prick, 'you always have a hard-on. For a change, I'd like to watch your cock become erect.'

'Your wish is my command,' he said.

I could imagine his smile, but I didn't look up. It wasn't his expression which interested me.

His manhood had already begun to grow. As the blood pulsed through his penis, the flesh rapidly became thicker, longer, and started to rise. I had often witnessed the reverse of this process because once he had shot his load, his maleness would start to diminish, gradually descending and shrinking.

But I was amazed at how fast he achieved an erection. He was leaning back against the open door of the fridge, and I remained on my knees in front of him. It was almost as if I had him pinned there, except that he had no wish to escape. I was as close as possible, my eyes at the same level as his swelling knob, not wanting to miss any detail. I watched in admiration as his male flesh rose up and up. For a moment his dick was horizontal, pointing directly at my face, like some kind of one-eyed serpent staring back at me.

I'd never really considered Peter's penis as a different creature, even though it often seemed to have an independent life of its own. Perhaps this could indeed have been the serpent which had tempted Eve, and I could well understand how she had succumbed, charmed by the discovery of another kind of paradise.

The alluring flesh continued its impressive ascent towards the vertical, but Peter wasn't the only one who was becoming aroused. My nipples were already hard, and I could feel a warm glow deep within as my cunt became damp and my clit started to dilate.

I watched as his knob stretched up and up, the foreskin drawing back and unfolding as the glans pushed its way even higher, until his impressive tool finally attained its maximum dimensions. The thick purple veins pulsed with vitality. Only a few inches away from Peter's erection, I could not fail to smell the potent aroma of male sexuality – and I wondered what to do next.

I glanced up at him, but I already sensed what he wanted me to do. He was still holding the carton of milk in one hand, but now his other hand came down on to my head, and he ran his fingers through my hair. His hand moved over my crown to the back of my skull. Very, very gently, he directed my face towards his virile flesh. He didn't try to force me, because he knew I would have refused, but he made sure I got the message.

It would have been very simple to lean forward,

to run my tongue over his penis, licking all the way up the stretched skin from the root to the domed head, then opening my lips to engulf the shiny glans and swallowing as much of his flesh as my mouth could take. I'd wanted something different, and here was the perfect opportunity. It was so tempting . . .

I was still looking up, Peter still looking down.

'Say *please*,' I said.

'Please,' he whispered.

'Louder,' I told him.

'Please,' he breathed.

'Beg me,' I ordered.

'Please,' he begged.

'No!' I laughed.

I turned my head and leaned back, managing to break the phallic spell which had enthralled me. As I looked away, something familiar in the refrigerator caught my eye. It was an aerosol dispenser of whipped cream. I remembered when I was younger how I'd had a lot of fun with one of those, squirting cream all over a cake and then over every edible thing I could find in the kitchen. I reached inside and took the container from the shelf. It was time for more fun.

'What's that for?' asked Peter, as he noticed what I'd found.

'Could spray it in the coffee instead of milk,' I suggested.

It was cylindrical in shape, the same length as Peter's knob but much thicker. I held it in one hand, sensuously stroking it with the other, rubbing my fingers up and down in exactly the same way they had so often glided over Peter's dick. I ran my palm over the rounded plastic cap, then brought it towards my mouth and slid out my tongue, slowly licking all across the dome before opening my mouth wide and slipping it between my lips. Glancing up, I saw Peter gazing at me. Then I pulled the cap off with my teeth and spat it out.

'Or how about it somewhere else?' I added.

I pointed the nozzle towards his cock, and I rubbed my thumb across the button at the top; it was like aiming a weapon at him, as if I was about to squeeze the trigger – and he would have been the most willing of victims.

He wished that I would, but he said: 'You wouldn't!'

Perhaps it was because I was so close, or perhaps it was because of what I was doing – and what I might do – but his cock seemed larger than ever before, throbbing in eager anticipation. And I could scent his heady male odour more strongly now, the most powerful aphrodisiac of all.

'Maybe I wouldn't,' I agreed, and I turned the nozzle towards my parted lips.

Then I pressed the button, and a thick jet of cream shot straight into my mouth. I squeezed and squeezed, changing my aim and directing the spray all around my lips, only stopping when my mouth was full, my lips coated. It was icy cold but very sweet. I let some of it ooze from my mouth, dripping down on to my chin. I caught it on my fingers, sliding them into my mouth and licking them completely clean, running my tongue across my lips and drawing in all the loose drops. Then I struck out my tongue one final time.

Peter was watching, gazing at my tongue which was white with whipped cream. I drew it back in, swallowed, and he licked his own lips. If anything, his cock had become even harder, even bigger. It seemed that he could ejaculate at any moment.

'You need cooling down,' I told him – and I turned the spray on his knob.

He gasped with surprise and pleasure as I coated every inch of his throbbing prick with a thick layer of white foam. I sprayed up and down, from his balls to his glans and back again, even over his stomach and thighs, until the container was totally empty. He'd caught his breath as soon as I started, and he didn't start breathing again until I'd finished decorating his cock.

I looked at him, he looked at me. I smiled, he smiled. We both laughed.

'You're crazy,' he said.

'I'm crazy? You're the one with whipped cream all over your prick! But it looks better like that.'

'Thanks a lot.'

'It looks good enough to eat,' I said.

I reached out with my right hand. Although the target was camouflaged, my index finger instinctively found the base of Peter's cock. I ran my finger up his length, blazing a trail through the foam, all the way up to the tip. Then I started at my fingertip and the pyramid of foamy white it had collected.

'The cream, I mean,' I added, and I slid my finger between my lips.

This time I seemed to taste more than just whipped cream. The stuff had been on his flesh for only a few seconds, but I was certain it was already penis-flavoured. The taste was absolutely irresistible.

I didn't want to do it.

But I found myself leaning towards Peter's prick.

Reason and judgement commanded me to stop.

My mouth opened.

Passion and lust were stronger than my willpower.

My hand took hold of his knob, guiding it towards my lips.

My tongue snaked out, licking away the cream which covered the glans, turning it from white to purple – and drawing it towards my eager mouth.

And his tool slid between my lips.

He was inside me for the first time.

It was as if I was helpless to prevent what was happening – but I no longer wanted to resist.

This was none of my doing – but it was exactly what I most desired.

Having sucked the first inch of solid male flesh between my lips, I paused, savouring the wondrous texture of what I had drawn in. I ran my tongue all across the head, over the smooth dome and around the ridge at the base, venturing further down to where the foreskin had drawn back, then back up, probing the slit at the apex with the tip of my tongue.

The whipped cream was cold, but his flesh was burning hot. I slid my lips further down, pretending I was trying to lick off as much cream as I could, yet knowing that I really wanted to fill my mouth with as much cock as was possible. My hand fed his length between my lips, inch by inch, until the tip touched the roof of my mouth. I sucked with my lips, slurped with my tongue, nibbled with my teeth and rubbed the glans across the inside of my cheeks.

Then I felt his tool sliding back over my lips, and it seemed that Peter was trying to deny me my prize. I brought my teeth together around his flesh, trying to keep what I had won and warning him not to retreat. His response was to push his knob back, deeper into my mouth. But then he began to withdraw again, and this time I realised what was happening. I had claimed his cock, but Peter was not accepting this passively; he was fucking my face . . .

He was slowly sliding his penis between my lips – and I wished I had a mirror so I could see everything. I wanted to watch his hard knob slipping in and out of my mouth; I wanted to see my own face, my own mouth, my own tongue as I performed fellatio for the first time; and I also wanted to watch Sweet Lips cock-sucking.

Peter's manhood was the finest meal I had ever tasted. No matter how delicious, this enjoyment wasn't merely oral, because my entire body was enjoying the unique banquet. I'd often felt a warm glow suffusing my whole being while I wanked Peter, like the first glimmerings of my own orgasm. The sensation had never kept escalating the way it did when I stroked my clit, building up towards a climax of my own. But now it did . . .

Without even touching my cunt, I was rapidly approaching an orgasm. Sucking cock for the first time was so erotic that I could sense the climactic rhythm rapidly welling up within my core, spiralling higher and higher, ascending towards its imminent release.

Peter was forgotten. He was nothing, as if the

flesh between my lips was mine, not his. All I cared about was hungrily devouring what was within my mouth, licking it as if I were licking myself.

I was aware of his hands on the side of my head, stroking me, but then I realised that instead of encouraging me to swallow him even deeper, Peter was trying to push me away. He had ceased gently rocking his hips to and fro, slipping his length between my lips. But I refused to surrender his knob, and I gripped it with my teeth. It was mine, I deserved it, I needed it. I had to keep licking and sucking his prick because that was the only way I could achieve ultimate satisfaction.

Then I felt the solid flesh between my lips twitch and throb, and a sudden fountain of warm liquid burst against the back of my mouth, trickling down my throat.

In my surprise, I opened my mouth and Peter succeeded in drawing his cock from my lips. He had ejaculated into my mouth, and that was what he had been trying to warn me about a moment earlier.

I didn't let him escape, my hand was still wrapped around his dick. As he pulled back, I leaned further forward, my mouth wide open, tongue out. I caught his next burst of semen on my tongue, and the taste boosted me higher. Tugging on his tool, I brought it against my mouth, rubbing the head across my upper lip just as it spunked again. I stroked the glans all around my mouth as if it were some kind of exotic lipstick. There was another shot of hot semen against my face – which rocketed me into orbit . . .

'Aaaaaaaaaah . . .'

I sank down on to my heels, feeling totally

drained. It was as if every bone in my whole body had dissolved, that I had no more substance than the warm come which dripped from my chin. I attempted to wipe the sperm away, but there was no co-ordination in my limbs. When my fingers tried to obey my brain, they were unable to.

I was totally weak and exhausted, yet I felt good, so good, the way I always did after an orgasm.

'White, no sugar?' said Peter.

'What?'

'Your coffee.'

I gazed up at him. He was grinning, which was no surprise. His knob had dropped down to the horizontal. It was shining wet with cream and spunk and saliva.

'Don't stir it with that,' I told him.

He opened his mouth to reply, then suddenly turned his head as though he'd heard something. He had, because then I heard it too. The front door.

'Shit!' He bent down and rapidly started to pull up his jeans.

As I wiped at my face with the palms of my hands, footsteps came along the hall towards the kitchen.

'What are you doing?' said a voice.

It was Lynn. The open door of the fridge covered Peter to the waist, and so she couldn't see him hurriedly tugging his denims over his half-erect knob. I was completely hidden; she couldn't see me at all. I wiped my sticky hands on Peter's jeans.

'What am I . . . er . . . doing?' he said, as he fastened his buckle.

I hoped he'd think of something quickly, hoped that Lynn would leave the room, hoped that I could sneak out of the back door.

'That's what I said: what are you doing?'

'Making coffee,' he answered. 'Er ... yes, making coffee.'

'Two cups?'

'Er ...'

'One's for me,' I said, peering from around the refrigerator door.

'What are you doing down there?' she asked.

'Picking up this,' I said, as I stood up and showed her the container of whipped cream.

Lynn looked from me to Peter, Peter to me. She knew something had been going on – and perhaps she even knew what.

'Want some ... er ... coffee?' Peter asked her. He was still standing behind the fridge door.

'Okay.'

I noticed that he still hadn't managed to zip up his jeans. There was whipped cream around the crotch, and smears of spunk on both his thighs from where I'd dried my hands.

'I'll do the coffee,' I said.

'Yeah ... er ... I've just got to ... er ... go upstairs a minute.' Peter pretended that something on the far wall took his interest. He walked towards the corner, then circled the table, keeping his back to Lynn all the time, and he headed for the door.

Lynn watched him go, then shook her head. She sat down at the table and looked at me.

'What's that you've got on the side of your face?' she said.

My hand immediately went to my cheek.

'Other one.'

I stroked my other cheek, felt something wet and sticky on my skin, and I rubbed it off with my finger. Luckily, it was white and came from an aerosol. I licked my finger.

'Cream,' I explained.

Lynn nodded. 'That's what I thought.'

I turned to make the coffee. My pulse was still racing, my skin was glowing with post-orgasmic radiance. At least I hadn't been naked when Lynn arrived, but I was convinced she must have known I'd just been licking dick.

'I'm glad you're here,' she said, 'because I wanted to ask you something.'

'Ask me what?'

'Would you like to be a bridesmaid?'

'A bridesmaid?' I turned and looked at her. It was such an odd question. 'Why? Is someone getting married?'

'Yes,' said Lynn. 'Me.'

It was true, Lynn was getting married. To Michael. (He was always 'Michael', never 'Mike'.) And they were marrying because they wanted to, not because they had to.

'You should come on honeymoon with us,' she suggested. 'You could be my wedding present to him.'

'Great,' I said. 'That's always been my ambition, to be a wedding present.'

'You could also be *my* wedding present.'

'Now you're talking!'

We both laughed. Several days had gone by, and we were on one of our breaks at work. There were just the two of us sitting together.

'Anyway, what's the answer?' asked Lynn.

'What? You really want me to go on honeymoon with you?'

'Three in a bed, why not? It's great fun.'

'You'd share Michael with me?'

'You can have Michael, I'll have his cock.'

'But you've already had it. You can't fool me. I was in the back of the car when you first fucked each other, remember?'

'How could I forget?' She smiled, remembering.

I waited for her to continue, but she didn't. She had never told one of her entertaining erotic stories about Michael; she had never even said she was still seeing him.

'What's the answer?' she asked again. 'Will you be my bridesmaid?'

'Yeah.'

'You don't have to be so enthusiastic!'

'Oh, yes, Lynn, I'd be absolutely delighted to be your bridesmaid. It's what I've always dreamed of.'

'That's better.'

'What do I have to do?'

'The most important thing is to help me choose the wedding dress.'

'I knew it would involve shopping!'

'That's the only reason I'm getting married, so I can buy some new clothes. My parents want a church wedding, the traditional ceremony, big reception, that kind of thing.'

I suspected it was also what Lynn wanted. 'Doesn't your mother want to help choose the dress?' I said, hoping I could get out of it.

'Yes, she does – although I don't want to go shopping with her. But I think she's worried that I might buy a see-through minidress.'

'You mean you won't . . .?'

'I'll make do with a see-through nightdress for the honeymoon.'

'In that case, I'll definitely come on the honeymoon!'

'You'll have to get all dressed up, too,' she added.

'I knew there'd be a catch.'

'We choose my dress, and we get one for you that goes with it. Don't worry about the price, my father's paying. We just go along, order whatever we want, complete new outfits for both of us, and you can buy yourself a present – something really expensive and totally unnecessary.'

I couldn't think of anything worse than having to buy clothes, although I felt pleased that Lynn had asked me to be her bridesmaid.

Before she could say any more, we were joined by some of the other girls.

'What's this I hear?'

'You're getting married, Lynn?'

'Not you!'

'Who is he?'

'What's he got that the others haven't?'

'He must have ten inches at least!'

Lynn replied: 'Yes, I'm getting married. His name's Michael.'

'Who?'

'Never heard of him.'

'Tell us about him.'

'Tell us about his cock!'

'There's nothing much to tell,' she said, which must have been the exact opposite of the truth.

'Perhaps she hasn't fucked him yet.'

'No sex before marriage, Lynn?'

'Or at least not with her husband!'

We all laughed, even Lynn.

'Sex before marriage?' she said, and she looked at us all in turn. 'I'd only agree to that on one condition.'

'What's that?'

'As long as it doesn't make me late for the wedding.'

CHAPTER NINE

Lynn was to be married in white.

'It's my favourite colour,' she said. 'It doesn't show the spunk.'

Things had happened very quickly because Lynn and Michael wanted to marry as soon as possible. They had found a house to move into, but they would only live together once they were married. It was difficult to believe she was the same girl I'd first known, the one whose whole life seemed dedicated to the pursuit of as much cock as possible.

If I hadn't been in the back of Michael's car that night, I would have totally disbelieved every one of Lynn's wild and horny stories.

I ought to have suspected something different was going on, because after our first night together – when she'd met Michael – I never again saw her try to pick up a guy. We didn't go out much, and I later discovered that she only invited me out when Michael was away. And since that first night, I hadn't seen Michael again. I could hardly remember what he looked like, but I'd see him soon enough at the wedding.

That would also probably be the next time that I saw Peter. Since first swallowing his spunk, I hadn't called round to see him again. It wasn't that I was avoiding him, but somehow I never found the time to visit. Whenever I went to the house, it was to see Lynn – and to go shopping.

I'd never imagined how much time it would take to choose a wedding dress, to be measured, to have fittings. This would have been total aversion therapy for the most addicted shopaholic, and it was absolute hell for me. Once Lynn had decided what she wanted, I was past caring what I wore. Rather than have to go through the whole process again, I'd willingly have been a nude bridesmaid. Lynn probably wouldn't have approved, however, because it was her wedding day and every eye was meant to be on her.

And every eye would be on her, because she looked truly stunning in her bridal gown. The skirt was composed of layer after layer of taffeta, all lace and frills, so long that it brushed the ground. The bodice fitted closely around her breasts, but she was concealed up to the neck – and even higher, because she also wore a veil which covered her face. Not an inch of her skin would be visible, because her gloves began where the sleeves ended. The veil would be removed once she reached the altar, her left glove removed to accept the wedding ring.

She looked magnificent, as she ought to have done considering the exorbitant price her father was paying for the gown. It seemed such a complete waste of money for something which would be worn for only a couple of hours. Even my own outfit cost almost as much as I earned in a month. It was similar to Lynn's, although on a much smaller scale. There were fewer layers and not as many frills, but I was still covered from neck to ankle, although at least I didn't have to wear a veil.

I stared into the mirror, hardly recognising myself. The white dress was so unlike anything I'd previously worn that I almost felt like a different person. I had to admit that I did like what I saw, if only because it made such a great change from my usual outfit of jeans and T-shirt, or the overall I wore at work. I found myself thinking that maybe I ought to buy myself some new clothes – and I wondered if this was the first sign of addiction.

I glanced at Lynn, thinking of what she'd said. She might only ever wear her wedding dress once, but I was sure she'd be very careful not to get spunk on it.

'You look like an angel,' said Lynn, as she studied me.

We were both in the fitting room, checking the last details of our outfits. Even before she'd put her dress on, Lynn had spent ages examining each seam, each button. Then I'd had to double-check everything once she was wearing it.

'My hair's the wrong colour,' I said, 'and I need some wings.'

'White looks so innocent,' said Lynn, 'so we ought to wear the sexiest undies we can find. Agreed?'

'Whatever you say.'

I'd long ago hit my shopping threshold. Lynn could have taken me to every department store and clothes shop in town – as she already seemed to have done, several times – and I would no longer mind. She next took me somewhere that we hadn't yet visited, a shop which sold nothing but exotic lingerie.

Once again, I was astonished by the cost. This was a different world. The smaller or more flimsy an item, the more astronomical the price. But it wasn't only the expense which amazed me, it was the garments themselves which were so fantastic. Panties that were totally transparent, others which were cut away so that the crotch was completely open, and others which consisted of nothing but the merest triangle of skimpy fabric which was tied by slender threads. Bras with holes through which the nipples could protrude, and those which didn't even get as high as the nipple. Nighties so wispy they could have been folded into a matchbox. There were garments I couldn't even recognise and didn't know the names of, such as sleeveless satin T-shirts which barely reached down to below the boobs, and something which resembled a swimsuit, except it was made of lace and never meant to go in water. The store was a wonderland of weird garments.

'Women really wear these things?' I asked.

'Of course,' said Lynn.

'But why?'

'So you can take them off.'

'Then why bother?'

'For men, to turn them on. Dress yourself up, then get undressed. It's like gift-wrapping a present.'

I knew what she meant. The first exotic underwear I'd ever seen had been what Lynn wore: the black lacy briefs, the front opening bra. And I'd immediately gone out and bought something similar – partly for myself, but just in case I had the chance to peel them off for Peter.

'They also make me feel good,' she added. 'Satin againsts my tits, silk against my crotch. Only the best. It gives me confidence somehow.'

'So what are you going to wear?' I asked, glancing around the store.

'And you,' she told me. Her eyes also examined what was on display. 'How about black leather?'

'What? Leather knickers!'

'Why not? All white and frilly and pretty on the outside, just like angels, but beneath that – a couple of tough bitches. Leather briefs with a zip up the crotch!'

I'd have laughed at the idea, except that I could see such a garment on display. Made of shiny black leather, the zip ran all the way down the front, around the crotch and up the back. This must have been so the wearer could fuck without taking it off.

'They hold special fashion shows just for men,' said Lynn. 'Guys come here, and a couple of models parade up and down wearing this stuff.'

'Or not wearing it,' I said.

'Exactly. Men buy these things for their wives and girlfriends.'

'But they're really buying for themselves?'

'Let's try some of it on.'

There was no way I could get out of it, and so we started sorting through the racks of bizarre garments. The salesgirl asked if we needed any help, but I let Lynn do all the choosing. She could find what she wanted very quickly, she was such an expert. It was her wedding, after all; and she had the money.

Arms full of bits and pieces, we went into the

same changing booth. After spending so long having our wedding outfits fitted, we seemed to have spent more time together in our undies than we had fully dressed. Lynn slid the curtain closed, and I noticed that each of the other three walls was made up of mirrors.

Because two of the mirrors faced one another, they also reflected the image caught by the one opposite – which meant there was a whole series of mirrored reflections, each one smaller, further away. I could see a whole infinity of my other selves vanishing into the distance.

'Stop looking at yourself,' Lynn told me. 'Get your clothes off.'

'The story of my life,' I said, and I started to unfasten my blouse.

Lynn peeled down to her bra and briefs, then put on what seemed to be a black corset. I couldn't understand why, because she didn't have any spare flesh around her middle.

'What is that?' I asked, watching as she fastened the row of hooks down the front.

'A basque,' she replied.

To me, underwear had always been a pair of panties – something that went around my bum, covered my crotch. When I grew up, and when my boobs grew, I'd added a bra. But a basque didn't cover either of the two vital areas of female anatomy. What Lynn wore started below the breasts and stopped above the crotch.

The basque supported her tits, which fitted into the half-cups at the top. Stocking fasteners hung from the lower edge of the garment, and Lynn reached for a pair of fishnets, which she carefully pulled over her feet and ankles, up her calves and thighs, then fixed to the suspenders.

'How do I look?' she asked, gazing at herself in one of the mirrors.

'Odd,' I said. 'Even odder than usual.'

'The bra doesn't go,' she said, as she ran her hands over her breasts. 'So it'll have to go.'

She reached behind, unhooked her bra and took it off. Her tits were held by the basque, which wasn't quite high enough to hide her nipples.

I looked at her bare boobs. Because of all the mirrors, there was no way I could avoid looking even if I'd wanted to. It was the only time I'd seen Lynn's bare breasts since the first night I went to her house. As I watched, I saw her nipples become hard. My own also began to dilate.

Strawberry, I remembered, and raspberry ...

'Your turn,' she told me.

'I'm not trying on one of those.'

'Why not?'

I couldn't think of a good reason, and so I accepted another basque from her, put it on and fastened it up. It was too loose, so I tried a different size. This was white in colour and it fitted, or almost; it was a tight squeeze and pushed my boobs up very high. I looked at myself in the mirror. Lynn was right, I realised, a bra wasn't meant to go with it. So I took mine off, and it was her turn to study my bare breasts.

'What do you think?' she asked.

'I'm not sure,' I said, and I shrugged. I watched as my tits jiggled, turning so I could see myself in all three of the mirrors. There were three reflections, three other selves, three Sweet Lips, all bare-breasted, half-clad.

'Would you wear something like that under your clothes?' Lynn asked.

'I wouldn't wear it without my clothes!'

'Think of the thrill, looking so respectable, but being so indecent beneath. Here, try the stockings on.'

I pulled on the black net stockings, the first time I'd ever worn any. I pushed the suspender straps down inside my panties, but had trouble fastening the stockings to them. Lynn helped me. Bare-boobed and high-heeled, in basques and stockings, we stood side by side, examining ourselves and each other. She looked good – and so did I.

'I know what you mean,' I said. 'It's like going out without your knickers on. You know you've nothing on, but no one else does.'

Her eyes met mine in the mirror. 'Didn't I once say that to you?'

'Probably.'

'We can't wear these panties,' she said. 'Got to be silk, at least.'

We were both in simple cotton briefs, hers black, mine bright red.

'Or maybe no knickers at all,' I said. 'Think how hot we'll be in our wedding outfits.'

Lynn thought for a moment and nodded. She was so attractive that I couldn't help staring at all four of her: Lynn and her images in the three mirrors. I could see her magnificent body from four different angles as she suddenly leaned down and removed her black panties.

I'd felt a brief thrill when she'd first discarded her bra, but that was as nothing to the jolt of excitement when she dropped her underwear.

My pulse began to race as I gazed at the reflection of her bare buttocks, so smooth, so taut. She stood upright again, and my eyes immediately focused on her crotch. Her pubic hairs were as white as her brother's.

'You're right,' she said, as she stood akimbo, gazing at herself in the mirror. 'This is what I'm going to wear underneath my wedding dress. Bare tits, bare cunt. Pity no one will see me like this.'

But I was seeing her; I couldn't keep my eyes off her.

'Michael will,' I managed to say.

'He's seen it all before.'

'You don't really want anyone else to see you like that – do you?'

Lynn said nothing. Her reflected eyes stared into mine, and her gaze moved down towards my crotch. She'd discarded her panties. I still wore mine. And I knew that she wanted to see me without them.

I felt strangely shy. If it had been Peter, I wouldn't have hesitated to drop my knickers. Even for another guy, I might have stripped off with hardly a second thought. When I'd first peeled off my bra in Lynn's room it had seemed quite natural; I'd thought nothing of it until she told me how daring I was. But now I realised how strange it was to undress for another girl – even though I wanted to . . .

Hooking my thumbs into the waistband, I pushed my red panties down my legs and stepped out of them. Lynn and I stood side by side, facing each other in the centre mirror.

All we wore were our shoes and stockings and

black velvet basques. Our breasts were bare, our nipples hard. Our pubic tufts were completely exposed, mine black, hers white. Lynn put her arm around my waist, and I did the same to her.

'We look as though we should be in a girlie magazine.' I said.

Lynn laughed. 'Yes, you're right. We're like a couple of sex sluts.'

Sex sluts. That was spot on. Lynn had the knack of finding exactly the right phrase – just as she'd invented *Sweet Lips*.

We were a sex fantasy come to life, I decided, two almost nude girls wearing exotic garments. From having read Peter's magazines, I now knew how lesbians could pleasure one another – and the male voyeur. Two girls having sex together seemed to be a predominant theme in such publications, both in text and photographic form.

The way Lynn and I were posing, it was almost as if we were about to stroke each other's tits, lick one another's cunt. I felt my pulse pick up speed again, and I tried to think of something else. But I could only think of our nude images.

'I can understand why they have pictures of naked girls,' I said. 'But why do they nearly always have their shoes and stockings on?'

'I think it's because high heels make the legs more shapely.' Lynn gazed at her own legs.

'Even when lying down? But guys don't look at the girls' legs, do they? Just their cunts.'

'How should I know? I don't look at their cunts. I like reading the letters. All the girls are nymphomaniacs whose favourite drink is spunk, and all the guys have nine-inch knobs and always fuck at least two girls simultaneously.'

This sounded familiar. Very much like Lynn's stories, in fact.

'Imagine having to pose for those photographs,' she said.

She pouted, as if the mirror was a camera, thrust out her boobs, raised one of her legs and rested it on the chair where we'd piled our discarded clothes – and as she did so, I caught a brief reflected glimpse of pink. My heart skipped a beat because of the momentary exposure of her glistening vagina. Lynn laughed, not suspecting what she'd accidentally revealed.

'Why do they do it?' she continued.

'Who?' I asked. I was still remembering the enticing sight of her twat. 'Why do who do what?'

'The girls in those magazines. Why do they show their tits, flash their cunts?'

'I suppose it's better than working in a supermarket.'

'So you'd do it, would you?'

I shook my head, not meaning no, but because I didn't know what to answer.

Lynn removed her leg from the chair, turning around as she did so and thus depriving me of a second glimpse of the most intimate part of her anatomy. She started to open the curtain of the changing booth, and for a moment I thought she was about to expose us both to the whole shop, but she only looked through and said something to the sales assistant.

A minute later we had more to wear, black elbow-length gloves and black suede chokers around our throats.

'Sex sluts,' I said, and we both laughed.

'The idea must be to reveal what's normally

hidden, but cover up what's usually exposed. Wide open cunts, but the forbidden female zones are the ankles, the neck, the wrists.'

'Does it turn you on looking at yourself like that?' I asked.

'No.' Lynn shook her head. 'But it turns me on looking at you!'

'Are you really going to wear that under your wedding dress?'

Lynn nodded. 'Definitely.'

'I'm sure Michael will appreciate it – once he sees it.'

'Yeah, but . . .'

Lynn ran her palms over her bare tits, down the basque, on to her thighs, pushing her fingertips towards her crotch.

'But what?' I prompted.

'I want our wedding night to be very special, to give him more than ever before.'

'That's why you invited me on the honeymoon?'

She smiled, tugged at her white curls, then said: 'I was thinking of shaving off my pubes.'

'What!'

'It's something different, something new.'

'But you wouldn't shave your head, so why shave your crotch?'

'To give him a thrill. To give me a thrill!' She put her hands on her hips again, examining herself in the mirror.

'Your pubic hair is lovely,' I assured her. And it was. 'It blends so well with your skin it's almost invisible. If it was like mine, yeah, get rid of it. But yours . . .'

As I spoke, I reached down and lightly brushed

my fingertips over Lynn's pubic mound. I did it instinctively, without thought, just as if I'd run my fingers over the hairs on her head. Her pubic hairs felt soft and fine. Exactly like Peter's.

'Ahhhhh . . .' sighed Lynn, and I saw her whole body tremble at my touch. 'Don't, don't.' She shook her head. 'I'm almost a married woman.'

I drew my hand back, suddenly realising what I'd done, and another surge of blood rushed through my body. My cunt began to feel warm, the start of a familiar pleasant sensation deep within me.

I turned away, and Lynn had done the same. We stood back to back, but we could still see each other in the opposite mirrors of the booth. We seemed far apart, our countless nude images being reflected so many times. I remembered the night she had first fucked Michael, after which she'd left the car and walked me towards my house. Our eyes met, and I knew Lynn was thinking exactly the same thing.

We were both remembering the way our lips had touched, how we had kissed so passionately as our mouths locked together and our tongues embraced. That kiss had promised so much, but the promise had never been fulfilled. If one of us turned around within the next second, however, and if the other also turned to face her . . .

I watched as Lynn stroked her blonde pubic hairs again. But she made no other movement, and neither did I. Perhaps there wasn't much we could have done in a changing booth, but we would never know. We kept looking at one another's reflection, and then the moment was gone. We were no longer ensnared by our primitive lusts. Or perhaps Lynn never had been. I might have imagined it all, or she could have been playing a game.

'Maybe you're right,' said Lynn, as she pulled at one of her pubic curls then let it spring back into place. 'I'll leave my pubes for now. Michael likes tugging them with his teeth – and I like him doing it.'

She turned around to face me, and I also turned.

'But if he wants them shaved,' I suggested, 'you could get him to do it.'

'Good idea. I could buy him a shaving kit for his wedding present. He'll think it's for his face, but instead he can brush the foam all over my cunt, rub it well in, then shave me bare.'

'Maybe,' I said, slowly, 'although perhaps your original idea was best. Surprise him on your wedding night with a smooth twat. And if you want a volunteer to shave your cunt, here I am. It's a tough job, but someone has to do it.'

Lynn said nothing, she just stared at me.

'And you could shave me at the same time,' I continued, and I curled a clump of jet-black pubic hairs between my fingers.

'What . . .?' said Lynn.

Then, unable to keep my face straight any longer, I burst out laughing.

'Ha fucking ha,' said Lynn. 'Very funny.'

'I thought so,' I told her.

She smiled, and ran her fingertips through her pubic hairs yet again. It was obvious she liked doing this, and she liked me watching as she did it.

'I'll tie a ribbon here instead,' she said. 'A pretty

pink bow.'

'If you want some help tying it . . .'

She laughed, undid her stockings and unbuttoned the basque. It was the first time I'd seen another girl absolutely naked. Lynn had looked very attractive in her sexy undies, but she was even more seductive totally nude. As far as I was concerned, the more bare flesh the better.

'How about a sexy negligée for our first night of wedded bliss?' she asked, as she sorted through the stuff she'd selected. 'Something for Michael to rip off me in the heat of passion.'

She tried one on. It hung just below her crotch and was so transparent that it didn't seem worth wearing.

'Why not do the opposite?' I suggested. 'He'll probably expect something like that. So if you really want to surprise him, why not wear a long nightgown, made of thick cotton, plus a woolly nightcap?'

She frowned as she thought about it, and began to shake her head.

'Then it's up to you to turn him on,' I continued. 'Do you want him to fancy you, or what you're wearing?'

As I spoke, I kicked off my shoes, removed the gloves and choker, the basque and stockings, and examined my infinite naked selves in all three mirrors. Lynn was also watching me. I shrugged and my boobs bounced. She shrugged, and hers did too.

'That's a good idea, you know,' she said.

'I know.'

'A long thick nightie.' She nodded, then took off the short skimpy one she was wearing.

For the first time we were both absolutely nude together. Lynn looked me up and down, while I did the same to her.

'Sometimes I wish I was a guy,' she said.

Perhaps it wasn't a game after all, and if not for Michael everything might have happened differently.

'Don't let that stop you,' I told her.

She smiled, so did I. She touched her fingers to her lips, blew me a kiss, and then we put our clothes back on. I watched as her pubis vanished within her knickers, as her boobs disappeared within her bra, and I wondered if I'd ever see them again.

I did see Lynn totally naked once more, as we were getting ready on the day of her wedding.

The previous day had been Lynn's last at the supermarket. The other girls had tried to persuade her to go out to a club with them that evening, to celebrate both leaving work and getting married, but she refused.

'They only want to find me some guy to fuck,' she told me, 'and I can arrange that myself.'

'You mean Michael?' I said.

'Who else?' she replied, as if there had never been any other man in her life, any other cock in her cunt.

'As long as you're not late for the wedding.'

'I won't be,' she promised. 'We've both got lots to do tomorrow. Don't forget the beauty salon. I'll see you there.'

That was how her wedding day started, with both of us having the full treatment. Our bodies were cleansed and steamed in the sauna, then massaged and oiled. I could easily have got used to such luxurious pampering, and it was a real pleasure having someone else wash and style my hair. While that was being done, the manicurist was working on my fingers and painting my nails. I even had my toes done. The final stage was when our faces were made-up for us, and I simply sat back and surrendered to the powders and creams, the mascara and eye shadow, the rouge and the lipstick.

I almost expected there would be someone waiting to help us undress and put on our wedding outfits, but we had to do that for ourselves. Lynn and I were in a room in one of the town's top hotels. Her parents seemed to have taken over at least half of the place. They were staying there that night, as were a number of the wedding guests, and they'd even provided me with a hotel room.

Lynn and I got undressed, stripping off our ordinary clothes, being very careful of our hair and make-up. At first we both tried to avoid staring at each other, but it was no use pretending we weren't interested in seeing one another nude.

'You didn't shave them off?' I said.

'Doesn't look like it,' she said, tugging at her blonde triangle.

'When does the ribbon go on?'

'When everything else comes off.'

We put on our basques and stockings, and looked at each other one final time. I admired Lynn's beautiful body, and I could tell that she was as appreciative of mine.

'Sex sluts,' I said, and we both laughed.

'You'd better help me on with my dress,' said Lynn.

'Michael's a lucky man,' I said.

'That's what I keep telling him!'

Lynn stepped into her wedding dress, and I stood behind her, carefully pulling it up over her stockinged legs and bare buttocks, up her back. As I guided her arms into the sleeves, my breasts brushed across her shoulder blades. I felt the warmth of her flesh against my bare boobs, and I remembered how her tits had once rubbed over my bare back. My nipples immediately became hard. I stepped back and began fastening the back of the dress.

As soon as I'd finished, Lynn turned towards me, and her eyes focused on my dilated nipples.

'And somewhere there's a lucky man for you,' she said.

'What?' I said.

I knew what she meant, but it was something I'd never considered before. She was right, I supposed. One day I'd find a man to marry. It was what every other girl did. But I hoped that I wasn't like every other girl.

'I'd rather have dozens of lucky men,' I told her.

'I've had dozens. Dozens and dozens. But one is all you need. One guy, one girl. One cock, one cunt. It's the perfect equation.'

She helped me into my outfit, and we were both properly clad in our immaculate white dresses when there was a knock on the door. I went and answered it.

'Hello,' said the man standing in the hall. He was in his late twenties, not very tall, and he held a video camera. 'I'm here to film the wedding. My name's Richard.'

'Come in,' Lynn told him.

'You're the bride?' he said, as he entered the room.

'How did you ever guess?'

'When you've done as many weddings as I have, you develop a sixth sense about that kind of thing.' He lifted the camera on to his shoulder and studied her through the viewfinder.

'You want to film me now?'

'I'll be with you throughout the wedding, so we might as well start now. I need a few seconds for editing in later.'

'If you'd been here a few minutes earlier,' Lynn said, 'you'd have had something worth filming.'

'What was that?'

'We were getting dressed.'

'If you want me to film you getting dressed, I will.'

I looked at Lynn, she looked at me, and Peter kept looking at her through the camera. He seemed to be serious.

'You're going to be following me around all day?' she asked.

'That's the idea.'

'Filming everything?'

'Everything. This is the happiest day of your life, and because of this video you'll have a permanent record of it all.'

'Not of the most important part,' said Lynn, smiling.

'That can be arranged.'

We both looked at him. He lowered his camera. His expression remained unchanged, and he didn't seem to be joking.

'I can make a private tape of you and your husband,' he said. 'Or if you wish, you can hire my camera for your wedding night.'

'Really?' said Lynn.

'Really,' he said.

She didn't take him up on the offer.

Not very long after, Lynn and I climbed into the limousine which drove us to the church. Richard and his video camera were waiting when we arrived, and after that he was never far away. Michael was also waiting, standing at the altar. It was the first time I'd seen him since that memorable evening, but I hardly recognised him.

It was a very long day, and a lot happened. After the wedding ceremony came the reception and dinner at the hotel. There was a dance and party that evening, and the celebrations lasted until the early hours of the morning.

As soon as I could, I escaped from my wedding outfit and changed into my new party dress, paid for by Lynn's father. It was made of crushed velvet, bright yellow with a black belt. The top was low-cut, the skirt quite short. I studied myself in the mirror of my hotel room, bending over, leaning forward, jumping up, spinning around. Because the dress fitted so well, my nipples remained discreetly hidden, and my crotch and buttocks stayed modestly covered. The most that could happen would be for the top of my aerolae to peep out over the velvet, or a flash of creamy white thigh to be seen above my stocking tops. That wouldn't bother me, and it probably wouldn't bother any of the guys who happened to notice. And I knew that I'd be noticed.

I didn't need a bra or panties, but I kept on the white basque to hold up my black fishnet stockings, then went back downstairs to rejoin the festivities.

I talked and danced and laughed and drank, then drank and laughed and danced and talked all over again.

It was a great day, and I really enjoyed myself.

And I also fucked for the first time.

CHAPTER TEN

It was a wonderful dream, and I hoped that it wouldn't end, but reluctantly I felt my consciousness slowly returning.

I lay still, my eyes closed, and tried to work out what day it was. The alarm would sound soon enough if I had to get up for work. No, I remembered, it was Sunday. That was good. Then I realised I wasn't even at home.

I opened my eyes and stared up at the ceiling of the hotel room. It was a huge bed, very comfortable, and I'd slept so well. I wondered what the time was, but didn't really want to know. All I wanted to do was stay where I was as long as possible, enjoying the unaccustomed luxury.

As I rolled over, I noticed that my clothes were lying on the floor. The velvet dress, the basque, the black stockings, the shoes, they were all scattered across the carpet. That seemed odd, because I usually piled my discarded clothes together on a chair. I tried to remember taking them off last night, but I couldn't. In fact, I couldn't remember anything about going to bed. The last thing I recalled was sitting in the hotel bar, having a final drink. How had I got up to my room?

It didn't really matter, I supposed, and I closed my eyes again, hoping to recapture my lost dream. It had been an erotic fantasy in which I'd been kissed and licked all over, in which my entire body had been stroked and caressed. We'd rolled about in bed together, his body so hard, mine so soft. Then his hardness had finally entered my softness, and we'd fucked and fucked and fucked.

But as I drifted back towards sleep, I suddenly recalled that it hadn't been a dream . . .

I sat up in bed, instantly awake.

If it hadn't been a dream, then it had really happened.

But my conscious mind could remember absolutely nothing about it – except that it was true: it *had* happened.

When I went to bed last night, I hadn't been alone.

There had been a man with me, in this room, in this bed.

And we'd fucked.

This was fact, not fantasy.

One of the most important moments in my life had occurred last night, and I had no real memory of it. Everything had become as unsubstantial as the dream I'd first believed it to be.

I felt very strange, very very strange. It was as if I'd been physically present during my first fuck, but my mind had been elsewhere.

I must have been drunk, I thought, absolutely out of my skull. But as I considered the idea, I knew it wasn't the case. Although I'd had plenty to drink last night, I hadn't been totally incapable. My mind had been alert, my senses fully aware, and my unknown lover had not taken advantage of me. At the time, I'd known exactly what I was doing – and what was being done to me. It was just that I couldn't remember a thing about it the morning after.

Because what I'd assumed was a very sensuous dream had been so rapturously exquisite, I could only presume my first fuck really had been the totally magical experience that I'd once hoped for.

But what had happened . . .?

What had we done to each other? If I'd dreamed that I was being kissed all over, did that mean he'd licked my cunt? If so, I had no real memory of my first experience of cunnilingus. And if he really had tongued my twat, did I come? And what had I done to him? Did I suck his knob? Did he ejaculate into my mouth? Or had he saved his spunk so that he could climax when his cock was deep within my cunt? Perhaps he'd done both. When he fucked me, did I have an orgasm? How long were we together? A few minutes? A few hours?

He must have fancied me very much last night, because I knew how attractive I'd looked. But had he been even more aroused when I stripped off my dress and he saw the basque and stockings beneath? I was a fantasy come true, his own willing sex slut. Did we fuck like that the first time? Did all my clothes only come off when we screwed the second time – or the third? Was he on top of me? Was I on top of him? Did his dick slide into my twat while I was on my hands and knees?

And who was he . . .?

He must have been one of the wedding guests.

Had I danced with him? Had he bought me a drink? There had been plenty of dances, plenty of drinks, plenty of guys – too many of each to remember. Yet why should he have been one of the wedding party? There were plenty of other people staying in the hotel, and he might have been one of those. He could have been a guy I met in the bar, someone who bought me a drink, someone I liked.

It had to be someone I liked, of course, or else I wouldn't have let him into my room. I was convinced that it had been my decision to be seduced. If I hadn't chosen to allow him in, my dream memories would not have been so blissfully positive.

He could even have been one of the hotel staff, I realised. If someone I liked had bought me a drink, it might have been the barman.

There were so many questions, and I wasn't even sure that I wanted to know any of the answers.

Since sitting up, I hadn't moved an inch. But my head had started to spin, and not because of my previous alcohol consumption.

I kicked away the bed covers, gazing down at my naked body. It appeared exactly the same as it had yesterday. There was no way of telling that I was different. No longer a girl, I was now a woman.

I was no longer a virgin, and that was fine by me. The great hurdle which had been looming up ahead of me had now been overcome and lay behind. If I remembered who the guy was, if I knew his name, he would always have remained an important part of my life.

Because I didn't know him, I didn't have to think of him. It was over and done. If I couldn't remember, I didn't need to forget.

I picked up the TV control and switched on the set. It was Sunday morning, the worst selection of programmes in the whole week. Nothing was more calculated to make me get up; but I continued to lie in bed a little longer, staring at the screen and trying not to think of anything.

It was only later, a long time later, that I realised how much my first fuck resembled the first episode of a new TV series. Often the best programmes were not very memorable when they began. But as time went by, their unimpressive origins were forgotten. Such shows kept getting better and better, as new scripts were developed and more interesting characters were introduced. And that was what was to happen in my own life, when my personal plotline produced plenty of new characters for me to fuck.

I rolled out of bed and went into the bathroom, where I gazed at myself in the mirror. My make-up was smeared and streaked, my hair a mess. I filled the bath and climbed into it, sinking down into the hot soapy water. Most times when I took a bath I ended up masturbating, but this morning I didn't feel the urge to lazily stroke my labia and luxuriously finger my clit.

Perhaps it was because that had all been done for me the previous night. That, and far more.

The only thing I wished I could remember was his cock . . .

After my bath, I didn't want to go downstairs and face anyone else, so I called up room service and ordered breakfast.

Lynn and Michael had already left for their honeymoon. Although it had been their wedding night, they'd already shared many nights together. Instead it had been I, the bridesmaid, who had enjoyed the bride's traditional first night consummation.

There might have been someone in the dining room who knew me, even if I didn't know him. If I saw my mystery lover, there was a chance that I would recognise him; but I'd already decided I didn't want to. It was no use looking back, I had to look forward.

And what I was looking forward to was another fuck.

Because my carnal initiation hadn't been at all memorable, I wanted to do it again. I needed to experience the ultimate pleasure of the flesh as soon as possible.

I knew exactly where there was a cock waiting for me.

Peter was still in bed, still asleep. He'd been one of the guys I'd danced with last night, one of those who'd bought me a drink – but he was definitely not the one who'd fucked me.

I was in trainers, jeans and T-shirt, and I did what I usually did when I was with Peter: I took them off. Although I stood naked next to him, there was no reaction. Even when I leaned over him, my nipples half an inch from his face, he kept on sleeping. I decided to reverse the usual routine. Opening my bag, I slipped on the black fishnet stockings and fastened myself into the white basque. Peter still made no response.

Carefully, I pulled away the bedcovers and

looked down at Peter's naked body. He was lying on his back, and he looked very young and very innocent. His limp cock seemed so small that I could have crammed every inch of it into my mouth, and probably his balls as well. I knelt down so I could examine his genitals more closely, and I was very tempted to suck his knob between my lips. I wondered what it tasted like when it wasn't covered with whipped cream.

I stretched out my right hand, rubbing my fingertips across the warm flesh. The instant I touched it, his prick started to uncurl, like a sleeping animal awakening and stretching. I glanced up towards Peter's face. He was either a brilliant actor or still fast asleep.

His cock grew between my fingers, becoming longer, thicker, harder. I stroked it with my hand, feeling it pulse with vitality. When I cupped his testicles in my other palm, they drew up, becoming tighter.

Peter must have had plenty to drink at the party yesterday, which was why he was in such a deep sleep. I wondered if it was possible to jerk him off while he still slept. Maybe I could even straddle him, slide his knob up into my cunt, then ride him to orgasm – preferably mine. His dream would be almost as fantastic as the one I'd had last night.

It was no use, I could hold back no longer. His nude body was so tempting, his growing cock so irresistible, and I leaned closer. Holding Peter's penis towards me, I opened my mouth and my tongue flickered out across the glans. At my touch, his tool grew even stronger. The foreskin had not drawn all the way back, but when I pushed at the taut skin with the tip of my tongue the head came totally free. I kissed the purple dome, tracing the ridge beneath with my wet tongue, bathing it in saliva.

The only time Peter had made me come was when his prick had been between my lips. He'd spurted his seed into my mouth, over my face, and his orgasm had triggered my own instant climax.

Now I could feel the first waves of heat burning deep within my cunt, as my labia began to moisten and swell, as my clitoris started to dilate. If I sucked Peter off again, I reasoned, then I would come again. My hungry mouth started to feed, lips sliding further down his length, tongue gliding wetly up and down the shaft.

That was when Peter woke up.

'What . . .?' he muttered, as he stared down at me.

I gazed up at him, but didn't say anything because my mouth was full. I paused for a moment, my lips and tongue no longer slipping over his cock flesh. The sight of his prick had hypnotised me, I realised, inflaming my female passions and provoking an urgent desire to fellate him. But I needed to regain control of my own body. Although I wanted to lick his dick, there was something which I wanted even more.

I needed something different, something new, and this was not it. I'd already done this. Sucking Peter's cock again would not advance my sexual education.

Reluctantly, I let the hard male flesh slither free from my lips, but I still kept a firm hold of his prick with my hand.

'Good morning,' I said.

'Don't stop, don't stop.'

He was too late, I'd stopped.

'Shall I get the whipped cream?' he asked, and he smiled. 'Or something else? Honey? Ketchup? What would you like?'

'You. That's what I'd like.'

'How did you get in here?' He rubbed at his eyes.

'I'm an angel,' I told him. 'I flew in through the window.'

He glanced at the window, as if taking me literally, then looked back at me. 'What are you wearing?'

'Not much.' I released his dick and stood up.

'I'm dreaming,' he said. 'You look great.'

'Thanks.'

'No, no, you always look great. But I've never seen you like that.' He looked me up and down, his eyes alternating between my exposed pubis and bare tits.

'I'm an angel,' I repeated, then added: 'And a sex slut.'

'This is a great way to wake up, far better than an alarm clock. What are you doing?'

I climbed on to the bed and slid one of my legs over his waist, kneeling above him. Reaching behind my back, I grabbed his hard cock.

'I've been your sex slut,' I said, as I gave his knob a single slow stroke. 'But now you're my sex slave.'

'I *am* dreaming!' He smiled again.

I shifted my weight forward, raised my right knee above his left shoulder, and brought it down. My left knee descended by the right side of his face, and I sat on his chest, my shins across his arms. He was pinned down, unable to move his arms and body; but if he had any sense, he didn't want to move. I released his prick.

'Remember when I licked your cock?' I said.

He smiled again. 'How could I forget?'

'Remember how much you liked it when I sucked and sucked and swallowed your come?'

'Yes.' He nodded.

'You really did like it?'

'Yes, yes.' He nodded twice.

'Now it's my turn,' I told him. 'It's your turn.'

I leaned forward, bringing my crotch towards his head.

'Do something I like,' I said.

Then I slowly stroked my cunt across his face, up his chin and lips, parting my inner labia over his nose, and on to his forehead, before rubbing myself back down again, gliding my clit all over his features.

It felt so good, and I sighed with total pleasure, rocking my hips forward again, sliding my vulva over his face, masturbating myself upon him.

Peter could do nothing except lie there. The only part of his upper body that he could move was his tongue.

As my twat slid once more over his mouth, I sensed his hot breath on my vaginal lips, and I felt something warm and wet probing blindly upwards. His tongue was searching for my clit, and I paused for a second or two to make his quest less difficult.

When he found his target, the unique touch of his tongue upon the most sensitive point of my entire body made every atom of my being quiver with total delight. I pushed back down, forcing myself hard across his mouth, sliding my cunt flesh over his lips. His stubbled chin massaged my buttocks, his nose stroked my pubis, and his tongue continued to tantalise my clit.

I was in paradise.

I rocked my twat to and fro, rubbing my labia over Peter's face. His mouth gently drew in my swollen clitoris, lips sucking at the delicate flesh, tongue tenderly caressing it towards the climax that I so desperately craved.

My movements became faster, more frantic, as I continued stroking myself across his wet mouth, while his tongue pushed ever harder, ever deeper, probing into and out of my cunt, tongue-fucking me.

I squeezed Peter's head between my thighs, pressed my vagina down over his mouth, forcing his tongue further and further within.

And then I came like I'd never come before, in a shattering climax which suddenly overwhelmed all of my senses. I was ablaze in a pyrotechnic inferno which totally consumed my whole body, a conflagration that destroyed everything I was or had ever been – but in which I was totally renewed, born again within a whole new spectrum of erotic sensations I had never even imagined could exist.

I leaned back on my heels, my heart pounding, my breath coming in short fast bursts. Every inch of my body was damp with sweat, but the wettest part of my body was my cunt. I felt warm drops trickle down the inside of my thighs, a mixture of Peter's saliva and my own come.

'Breakfast in bed,' said Peter, now that his mouth was free. 'What a great meal.'

He was still pinned beneath me, but I made no effort to release him. I felt so weak that it took all my strength to reach down and unhook my stockings.

'How about you?' said Peter.

I unfastened the front of the basque and let it fall to the floor. It didn't make me feel any cooler.

'Don't you want to eat?' he added.

I took a deep breath, raised each of my knees in turn, and freed Peter's shoulders and arms before sliding further down the bed until I straddled his waist. I reached behind, finding his erect cock, then raised my buttocks.

'Shut up and fuck me,' I said, and I aimed his shaft towards my cunt.

I lowered myself towards his maleness, lightly sliding the glans across my cunt, gasping with pleasure at the first wonderful touch, hesitating, then rubbing the dome over my clitoris, sighing at the delicious sensation, wanting to continue stroking my clit, but also needing his cock deep within me, directing it towards the heart of my femininity, gliding it between my inner labia . . .

Then his penis slid up into my cunt, and it felt absolutely sensational.

I didn't move, I didn't need to. Just having Peter's cock inside me was more than enough, and already I could feel the embers of my previous orgasm starting to glow again.

His hands were on my breasts, caressing them with his palms, stroking my nipples with his fingertips. He raised his hips, his knob slid even deeper into me, and another tremor of pleasure rippled across my body. He drew back, pushed up, drew back, pushed up.

I was being fucked.

It may not have been the first time, but it was the first time that I could remember, the first time that I could enjoy every magnificent moment.

As his hips thrust up, I pushed down, and his prick glided in deeper than ever before, rubbing across my clitoris, sliding between the walls of my vagina. When he moved down, I raised myself up, up, so that his shaft started to slip away through my warm wet flesh. But just as it seemed that his knob would escape my cunt, our hips rocked back together.

I wasn't being fucked; I was fucking. We were both fucking, sharing each other, sharing everything that we had.

And it was the most wonderful experience I had ever known.

That was almost my last thought before all my mental processes were engulfed by my impending climax. I realised that I was fucking for the second time – but for Peter this was the first time.

At that very instant he thrust himself within me, and his arms went around my body, pulling me close to him as he became still. He groaned as he climaxed, and his fiery eruption ignited my own orgasm. I felt his seed spurt inside my body, and simultaneously I came, burning up with ultimate rapture.

It was his orgasm, it was mine. We were as one, as close as two people could ever be to each other, and we held on very tight.

I wished I hadn't waited so long for this moment. Why had I never fucked before? Why hadn't I used his penis for its true purpose instead of jerking him off? I'd wasted so much time, so much spunk.

An eternity later, Peter whispered: 'That was . . . ' He shook his head, because words were not sufficient.

'Yes,' I agreed. 'It was.'

'Thank you.'

'And thank you.'

'You know what?'

'What?'

'You still haven't had that cup of coffee.'

'That's the only reason I keep coming back here.'

'Is it? In that case, you're never going to get a cup.'

'No coffee?' I said. 'Okay, then we might as well fuck again.'

I had all that lost time to make up for.

We were sitting up facing one another, my thighs spread over his, still embracing, his cock still within my cunt.

I rocked my hips up and down, but I could no longer feel his prick filling my twat. He had already begun to lose his virility. I clenched my vaginal muscles, squeezing his tool, and I continued attempting to ride him again. But my hips rocked too high and his dick slipped free. We both looked down, and Peter shook his head.

'You've worn it out,' he said. 'It needs a chance to recover.'

'No,' I said. 'I want it now.'

I pushed him back on to the bed, and I took hold of his knob in my hand. I'd never failed to arouse his manhood before, and I started to run my fingers across his male flesh. Although his prick ceased its descent, it didn't regain any of its lost rigidity.

There seemed only one thing to do, but first I climbed out of bed and wedged the wardrobe door open at the correct angle.

I peeled off my stockings and climbed back on to the bed, then I ran my right index finger along the length of Peter's hardening shaft several times, teasing him, tempting myself. Drawing my finger away, I lifted it to my lips, ran my tongue across the tip. I looked at Peter, he looked at me.

Then I went down on him.

He raised himself on one elbow so that he could watch what I was doing, and I was also watching. I stared in the mirror as Sweet Lips finally opened her mouth to suck in her lover's knob, while I did exactly the same to Peter's prick.

I could smell my unique female scent upon his male flesh. His cock was wet with come, his own and mine, a potent erotic mixture which tasted far better than whipped cream.

CHAPTER ELEVEN

Looking at other people's photographs was always boring, but at least I could flick through them quickly – unless I was given an even more boring explanation of every picture. I knew I wouldn't be able to ask Lynn to fast forward through her wedding video, which was why I kept finding an excuse not to visit her and watch the tape.

Finally, there was no escape and I had to see it. And most of it was as bad as I'd expected. The wedding had been dull enough at the time, but to see electronic repeats of rings being placed on fingers and three-tiered cakes being cut was almost more than I could bear. There were, however, some sequence which completely held my attention: the parts of the video where I could see myself.

Watching myself on screen was completely different from looking at myself in the mirror. The girl in the mirror had always been someone else; someone who raised her right arm if I raised my left, for example. In this respect, Sweet Lips was my exact opposite. But the girl on the video was different. Her right was my right, my left was her left. She was me, and it was as if I was watching myself for the first time.

I'd seen myself in photographs, of course, but this was not the same at all. I moved, I spoke, I was alive; I was far more than a frozen image on a piece of paper. My video image fascinated me as much as my reflection in the mirror had done when I was younger.

There had been another reason why I didn't want to watch the wedding video, which was that I might recognise the guy who had first fucked me. Not knowing who he was, at least I could tell myself that he was really special, the most fantastic guy a girl could ever meet. Which was true. Because on that night, to me, he had been both special and fantastic. But I didn't want my illusions shattered by discovering that he was totally ordinary.

If he was on the tape, however, I didn't see him; but that might have been because I was too busy watching myself.

A month had passed since the wedding, and it was the first time I'd seen Lynn. Needless to say, I'd seen Peter plenty of times. That first day we'd sucked and fucked, fucked and sucked for hours and hours – and we did the same the second day, the third, the fourth, and every other day that we were together, until it seemed there was nothing else we could do with each other, to each other, for each other. I enjoyed every minute, every second, but I began to realise even that wasn't enough. I wanted something else – and somebody else.

I'd no idea what that something was, or who that somebody else would be. All I knew was that it would happen.

And it did.

'You made the video for a friend's wedding,' I said.

'And you were the bridesmaid,' said Richard.

I was surprised that he remembered me, because the boots and jeans and sweater that I now wore were very different to my wedding outfit.

'You told Lynn that she could hire a video camera from you if she wanted.'

'That's right.'

'So can I hire one?'

'Of course,' said Richard. 'What for?'

'Isn't it obvious?'

'You want to make a video, I guessed that. If I know what sort, I'll know which camera to recommend.'

'The one you used for the wedding would be fine.'

'That's quite a complex piece of equipment. Have you ever used one before?'

'Yes,' I lied.

Richard nodded, knowing I was lying.

I was in his shop on the outskirts of town, where he sold various kinds of electronic and photographic equipment: stereos and computers, photocopiers and telephones, cameras and televisions. All of it was second-hand. I already knew that filming weddings could only be a part-time job. In fact, everything Richard did seemed to be part-time; his shop was only open half the week. I later discovered that he had lots of different occupations, doing whatever he could to make money. He could turn his hand to anything electrical or technical.

I wanted to make a video of myself; I wanted to

see what I looked like; I wanted more than the few brief glimpses of myself I'd seen during Lynn's wedding tape; I wanted to see myself in close-up, in both left and right profile; I wanted to see all of myself; I wanted to see myself naked . . .

'Do you want to film yourself?' asked Richard.

I stared at him. He'd known I was lying about previously using a camera, but how did he know what I wanted one for? Did most people hire cameras to film themselves? Perhaps they did. I'd only thought of the idea because Richard had mentioned that Lynn and Michael might want to make a permanent record of their wedding night.

'It's quite difficult,' he continued, although I hadn't answered him. 'You have to position the camera just right, make sure it's steady and at the correct angle, and you need to stay more or less in one position or else you go out of frame. A tripod is essential.'

'A tripod?' I said. 'Isn't that when three people go to bed together?' (I didn't know him well enough to say 'fuck', and I didn't want to lead him on. He wasn't my type.)

He didn't even smile.

'How long do you want the camera for?'

'A few hours, that's all. Overnight. How much?'

He shrugged. 'Not much.' He turned, picked up a video camera from the shelf next to him, studied it and shrugged again. 'Nothing.'

'Nothing?' I asked, immediately suspicious. Nothing always meant something – and I could guess what that something would be.

'It costs me nothing to lend you the camera.

You only have to pay for the tape.' Another shrug. 'And buy me a drink.'

Buying a drink meant going out with him, and he hoped that would lead to staying in with him. I said nothing.

'Shall I show you how to use the camera?'

'Okay.'

'Let's go through here,' said Richard, gesturing to the doorway behind him. 'Would you like a coffee?'

I laughed, and he frowned. I was thinking how long it had taken me to get a cup of coffee from Peter.

'Yeah,' I said. 'Why not?'

Richard locked the shop door, picked up a tripod from the corner, and I followed him into the back. The shop itself was very small, but it was much larger at the back, absolutely stacked with radios and speakers, computer monitors and printers, boxes and cartons, desks and filing cabinets. In the far corner was a metal staircase, and I followed him up. I wasn't very surprised to find myself in his flat; but what did surprise me was that he started making some coffee.

We were in his living room, and while the water was boiling Richard mounted the camera on the tripod and connected it to the television set.

'Sit down,' he said, aiming the camera at me.

I walked towards one of the armchairs, glancing at the TV set as I did so – and I saw myself walking towards one of the armchairs . . .

I stopped immediately and my image also stopped. Then I resumed walking and sat down, all the time watching myself on the television screen. When I raised my right hand, I did the same on screen. Richard moved away, leaving the camera aimed at me, and I just stared, seeing myself as I really was.

'You'll get bored soon enough,' he said, handing me a cup of coffee.

He was wrong. I was absolutely mesmerised and could hardly even remember telling him how I liked my coffee.

'The camera is linked up via the video recorder and the television,' he continued, 'but that's just working as a monitor. There's no tape in the machine and this isn't being recorded. If all you want to do is look at yourself, this is the way to do it. Or maybe you want to make a tape of yourself sitting in a chair, drinking coffee?'

I shrugged, and I watched myself shrugging.

'I'll show you how to use the camera,' said Richard. 'And if you still want to borrow it, you can.'

'You think I won't?'

'There's nothing as boring as seeing yourself on video.'

'Really?'

'It's just like looking in a mirror.'

That was what I hoped.

'It's okay if you're doing something,' he continued. 'Or if it brings back memories, like a holiday tape, for example.'

'Or a wedding tape?' I said.

'I'm not married.'

'That's not what I meant. Have you really made wedding night tapes?'

'Yes.'

'Filmed people fucking?' I was up in his flat,

drinking his coffee; by now I knew him well enough to say 'fucking'.

'Yes.'

'And?'

'And what?' He shrugged. 'And nothing. It's far more fun doing it than filming it.'

'It's a hard job, you mean, but someone has to do it?'

He almost smiled, but hid himself by looking through the viewfinder. 'Come here, I'll show you how to use the camera.'

I stood up, walked towards him, watching myself do exactly that on the television. My face suddenly became larger, filling the whole screen.

'That's the zoom,' explained Richard.

He was a very good teacher, being both an expert and an enthusiast. If anything, he took too long explaining every detail to me. I became impatient because all I needed to know was how to use the camera, not its technical specifications and every detail of its construction. Richard also acted as my model, standing in front of the camera as I learned all of its functions and practised its capabilities.

'Play with it as long as you like,' he told me. 'If you still want to borrow it, fine. See you later. I've got a shop to run.'

He headed back downstairs, leaving me with the camera and my own image on the TV screen.

It didn't take very long before I concluded that Richard was correct. Seeing myself on video was almost as boring as watching myself in a mirror – or in most mirrors. I'd never been bored in front of my own mirror, up in my own room, where Sweet Lips and myself had so much fun together.

If I took the camera home with me, I could do what I originally planned, tape myself as I peeled off my clothes and saw my true self naked for the first time.

I wished I was at home now, but then I wondered why I needed to wait. I was on my own, I had the camera, I could see myself here. All I needed to do was strip off. It would be far more of a thrill to undress somewhere new, I realised; it was much more daring to be naked in Richard's flat than to disrobe at home. As I thought about the idea, I grew more and more excited.

The camera had been moved as near to the television as possible, so that I could look straight into the lens and also see myself looking back from the screen. It was almost like watching myself in a mirror. If I stood far enough back, my whole body was in view. I checked the video recorder beneath the TV set, making sure that there really was no tape in the machine. Neither was the tape counter on the camera moving. It appeared that Richard had been telling the truth. Although I could see myself on screen, nothing was being recorded.

I left the room, heading back towards the top of the stairs. There was no sign of him, he was still down in the shop. I made my way back, stood in front of the camera, in front of myself on the television screen, and I took off my clothes.

There was no need to do a striptease because I wasn't trying to entice anyone except myself. In any case, I was in too much of a hurry; I just wanted to see myself naked, as I really was. Off came my boots, I thumbed down my jeans and briefs together, pulled the sweater over my head, unhooked my bra and let it fall.

I stood nude, gazing at my own body. For the first time I knew that it was myself I was watching, not Sweet Lips, not my best friend on the other side of the mirror.

Because I was subtly different from my reflection, it was as if I was seeing someone I almost recognised. But this person was also a stranger, and I could therefore view her objectively – notice how good-looking she was and admire the wonderful shape of her unclad body. I ran my hands over myself, watching myself, seeing my palms rise up over my thighs and hips, across my ribs and then on to my breasts. Stroking my bare boobs, feeling the nipples grow harder, watching them grow harder, it was almost like the television screen was a mirror. Except it was better than a mirror.

My left hand continued caressing my tits, but my right hand started to slide lower, lower, down towards the black thatch of pubic hairs, gliding through them, further down, deeper within.

And I did what I had so often done in front of my own mirror.

I began masturbating.

Even though I was enjoying far more orgasms than ever before, because Peter and I had been screwing regularly and he also often licked my cunt, I still frequently finger-fucked myself. If anything, the more climaxes I achieved, the more I craved.

And now I stroked my hand across my moist labia, rubbing my knuckles over my swollen clitoris, sliding my middle finger up into my twat.

As always, I enjoyed stimulating myself, and I enjoyed it even more because I could watch as I pleasured my nude body on television. Normally I would have been lying down, my eyes closed as I luxuriated in my own sensual seduction. Instead I was standing upright, my gratification heightened by watching the screen as I blatantly fondled my bare breasts and unashamedly caressed my cunt. The sensation was absolutely wonderful, and I quickly guided myself towards my peak.

While hedonistically stroking my intimate flesh, I found myself moving closer towards the TV screen. This was so I could see myself more clearly, but it also meant that I was nearer to the video camera – which had the effect of limiting how much of my body was visible on the screen. What was left of me became more and more enlarged, however, until the only part of my anatomy on display was my cunt.

The camera was focused on my twat, and my twat filled the screen. I'd never seen my vagina in such graphic detail, and for a few seconds I drew away my hand so that I could examine my genitals on television. Every moment that my fingers were away from my cunt seemed like an eternity. My climax was imminent, supreme satisfaction so close, and yet I delighted in teasing myself.

Then, when I could wait no longer, I allowed my fingertips to return to my cunt, opening myself to the camera so that I would miss not a single explicit detail of my explorations.

A single blissful stroke across my clit, that was all I needed and desired, and it was sufficient to send my whole being spiralling higher and higher, up into the ultimate paradise of orgasm.

And I watched every rapturous moment, watched every erotic detail, watched myself ecstatically come on screen.

Finally, slowly, I backed away, still looking at the television as more of my nude self came into view. I raised my hand to the screen, beckoning, but I wasn't doing that for my benefit. It was for the other person who had also been watching. Sitting in the chair, I waited for Richard to return.

It took less than a minute before he arrived back upstairs. When he entered the room, he looked everywhere except at me, but his eyes eventually gazed at my naked body on the TV screen.

'How did you know I was watching?' he asked, and it was as if he was talking to my television image.

'How couldn't you be watching?' I replied.

Everywhere was wired up, here in his flat, down in the shop. How many TV screens had I been on? Had Richard made a tape of me masturbating? I didn't know – and I realised that I didn't care.

He lifted the camera from the tripod, hid himself behind the viewfinder, and finally turned towards me.

'You asked me up here,' I continued, 'hoping I'd do what I did.'

'You did far more than I ever hoped,' he told me as he moved closer, bringing the camera closer.

I watched my naked body grow larger on the screen. The lens was aimed at one particular part of my anatomy, and I leaned further back in the chair, spreading my legs wider for the camera's voyeuristic gaze.

'You were too near,' said Richard, 'which meant your cunt was out of focus. Shall we go for a retake?'

I slid my hand down over my pubic hairs, slipping my index finger even deeper, feeling my wetness. Then I glanced towards the TV, watching as my cunt filled the screen.

'No,' I said, 'I've done that once. I want to do something else.'

The camera was very close to me, which meant that Richard was also very close. I removed my hand from my crotch and reached forward to unzip him. Both of his hands were occupied with the camera, so he couldn't have stopped me even if he wanted to. He didn't want to, although he backed away, retreating towards the tripod, trying to put the camera back into place. That should have been relatively easy, but he was distracted by me following and pulling his pants down.

I'd thought that Richard wasn't my type, but I was wrong. He had a cock, a hard knob, and that meant he was definitely my kind of guy. They all were . . .

He managed to fix the video camera back on to the tripod, and I managed to get his clothes off.

Then we fucked.

I was up against the wall, my legs wrapped around his waist as his penis slid in and out of my welcoming twat.

'How many times have you done this?' I breathed.

'Never,' Richard sighed, and with every

syllable he slipped his dick deeper into me. 'Never like this. But I've always dreamed of it.'

'That's what I'm here for,' I whispered. 'To make your dream come true.'

I gazed over his shoulder while I spoke, watching myself on the television screen as we fucked and fucked and fucked.

And my own dream had also come true because I'd finally achieved my ambition: I was a TV star.

CHAPTER TWELVE

Richard was right: my cunt was out of focus.

But next time it was he who held the camera, and he made sure that every detail of my twat was absolutely clear. It was an amazing experience to see myself masturbating on television, to study my own vagina as I became more aroused and achieved orgasm.

He had secretly recorded me the first time, then continued taping while we fucked. That was what he meant by his dream coming true: he'd always wanted to film himself screwing.

And after the filming came the first showing, which had led to us fucking once again. This could have lasted forever, I realised; each time Richard and I fucked, we made a tape, and each time we watched the tape we fucked again. It seemed like a great way to spend all of eternity.

He had video recorders and televison monitors everywhere. We could watch ourselves fucking at that very moment, doing on screen what we were doing to each other. Or Richard could be licking me out, while on screen I might have been on my knees drawing as much of his knob between my lips as I could. It was wonderful, better than being surrounded by mirrors, because all the different versions of myself would be doing different things simultaneously.

'So you'd never filmed yourself fucking?' I asked.

'I've tried to,' said Richard. 'I've set up hidden cameras a few times, rolled the tape, but something has always gone wrong.'

'Why hide the camera? Why not do it like that?' I gestured to the tripod by the bed.

We'd just fucked again, and the camera had filmed us again – we'd watch that film the next time we fucked . . .

'Not every girl is as willing as you,' Richard replied. 'Although I've found a few who were willing to do other things.'

'Like what?'

'Like getting undressed.'

'You've filmed girls undressing, but they didn't want to be filmed fucking?'

'There is quite a difference.'

I shrugged. 'Maybe.'

'It started with one girl. I wanted to film us screwing, but all I got on tape was the part where she took her clothes off.'

'So she didn't know you were filming her?'

'Not at the time, but then she noticed the camera.'

'What happened?'

'I thought she'd be furious, and she was at first. So was I, because we were about to fuck and didn't. Then she made me run the tape for her, and she was fascinated. She just loved watching herself, and she kept on watching herself while we screwed.'

I nodded, understanding how she had been

fascinated by her own body. While Richard and I fucked each other, it was always myself who I watched on screen – not him.

'After that,' he continued, 'she insisted I make another tape of her stripping off, which of course I was only too happy to do. But she wouldn't let me film us fucking.'

'What happened to the tape?'

Richard smiled. 'I sold it.'

'You *what* . . .?'

'I made some duplicates and sold them. That's how I make my living, as you know. I sell stuff.'

'What did the girl think about you selling videos of her stripping off?'

Richard shrugged. 'She never knew, or at least I don't think so. I only sold them after we split up.'

I glanced at the nearest television screen, where I was sucking Richard's cock while he tongued my twat.

I asked: 'So when you and I split . . .?'

'Would it bother you if other people saw that?' he asked.

This was something I'd never considered before. I hadn't minded when Peter first saw my bare tits, and I wouldn't care if anyone saw me naked. But what about naked on video tape? And what about naked and fucking? There was quite a difference between being nude in the flesh and licking dick on screen, I realised.

But so what?

Seeing myself turned me on, whether I was just naked or whether I was swallowing spunk – and so it would certainly excite and stimulate any guy who watched me on video.

'Why should it bother me?' I said.

'It wouldn't? But it would bother me! I don't want anyone to watch me fucking. Those tapes are for our eyes only.'

'Pity.'

'What?'

I laughed. 'Only joking,' I said – although I wasn't sure whether I was joking or not. 'But you've taped other people fucking.'

'No, I haven't.'

'The wedding night films you've made.'

'I haven't made any,' said Richard, shaking his head. 'I lied.'

'What about these other girls, the ones you filmed stripping? Have you got any tapes left, or did you sell them all?'

'Once you sell something, it's gone. Unless it's on video tape, when you can make copy after copy after copy – and sell copy after copy after copy. In theory, at least.'

'You've really filmed girls taking off their clothes?'

'Yes.'

'And sold the films?'

'Yes. The first one was made by chance, but after that it was all planned.'

'So the girls knew you were selling the tapes?'

'Yes. It was a job.'

'They were paid?'

'Yes. You've seen nude girls in magazines, these were just the same. They were like moving pin-ups. In fact, they were far more modest than most of the girls you can see in magazines. They didn't spread their legs and finger their twats. Or not very often.'

'You keep saying *were*.'

'It was a while ago, and there were only a few tapes. They were fun to do, but I never made enough money from them.'

'Can I see one of these films?'

'They're no great masterpieces.'

'That's okay.' I glanced over at the nearest screen, watching Richard's semen splash on to my breasts. 'I'd like to see one of your *other* films.'

Richard seemed reluctant, but I realised that was because he was enjoying the way I was fondling his balls and stroking his knob. We'd sucked and we'd fucked, and I was getting him ready to do it all again. By now I knew his penis better than I'd ever known Peter's prick. Peter was just a boy, but Richard was a man – and far more expert with his fingers and tongue and cock.

I released his shaft, letting him know there would be no more physical contact until he did as I asked. He bent down, trying to lick at my nipples. It was a great sacrifice, but I leaned away, moving my breasts out of his mouth's reach.

'If that's what you want,' he said, standing up. He went around the room, switching off the different video machines, and all of the screens blanked. 'But I'd much rather watch you than anyone else.'

I agreed with him; but I could see myself at any time. This was something new, and I always wanted something new.

He produced a tape, slid it into one of the machines, returned to the bed, then pressed the play button on the remote control.

'This is Dawn,' said Richard, as the screen flashed through a rainbow of colours. 'She reminds me of you. Although not as good-looking, of course.'

'Of course,' I said.

The screen showed a girl walking down the street. Her hair was as black as my own, but it was straight and hung halfway down her back. Although her features were completely different from mine, there was something about her which reminded me of myself.

Dawn was very attractive, I had to admit – the kind of girl that any guy would look at. I recognised the road where she was, part of the main shopping centre in town. If I'd ever seen her, I was sure I would have remembered – because it wasn't only guys who would look at her. Girls would stare at her too, their glances a mixture of admiration and jealousy.

She was wearing white high-heeled boots and a smart white suit, and these contrasted starkly with her flowing mane of long jet-black hair. The skirt was knee-length but slit halfway up the left thigh. The jacket was unfastened, and her blouse was tight across her breasts.

'My idea,' said Richard, 'was to try and make a film like this as realistic as possible. You see pictures of nude girls in magazines, but so what? They're always naked, they're total fantasy. But if a man sees a good-looking girl, he always imagines what she's like without her clothes. So my idea was to show the girl in real life, the way she appears in public, then show what she's like in private.'

'Makes sense to me,' I said, and it did.

'No,' said Richard. 'I was just too subtle.'

More than anything, the film reminded me of

watching an old silent movie, perhaps because it was so direct. It was in colour instead of black and white, but there was no dialogue or sound effects, although a music track had been added. It was short, there was no plot, and in a way it was like a documentary. A camera followed Dawn, recording exactly what she did.

And what she did was take her clothes off, which didn't seem very subtle to me.

All the time she behaved as if she was totally alone, never looking at the camera. She walked down the street, went in through a side door, up a set of stairs, into her flat and started to undress.

She stripped off gradually, walking around and doing various things between shedding each garment, until she was clad only in her white bra and briefs. As the bra came off, she turned and stood in front of a mirror, her beautiful boobs rising and falling while she combed her hair.

Then the camera focused on her buttocks, and the panties which were stretched across them. When she thumbed her tight knickers down, the camera followed as they slid over her shapely legs. Then Dawn was seen from the front, naked to the waist. Her right hand slipped down towards her crotch, but this was out of frame. She closed her eyes and smiled, and the viewer could only imagine that she was touching herself up.

I noticed that Richard was watching me instead of the video, but I supposed that was because he'd seen it so many times; then I noticed that my own right hand had slid towards my pubis. I was imitating the girl on television – which made a change from always doing what Sweet Lips did on the other side of the mirror.

The camera began to move down, following Dawn's hand; but just as her pubic hairs were about to come into view, she turned around and walked across the room. She made her way into the bathroom, turning on the bathtaps. The camera was close behind, studying the smooth curve of her buttocks, watching her breasts sway as she bent over the tub. Once the bath was full, she climbed into the water.

In all the other films I'd ever seen where a girl took a bath, she was always modestly covered in thick foamy bubbles. But not here. Here there was only water, and water is transparent. The camera was above Dawn, focusing on her face as she lay down. Then it gradually rose higher, slowly pulling back to reveal more and more of her naked body.

Her bare breasts came into view, the nipples standing out above the water which lapped over her boobs. Finally her pubic mound appeared for the first time, the black hairs in stark contrast to the whiteness of her flesh. Her pubis was like a tropical island thrusting out above the ocean, constantly overwhelmed by tidal waves; her pubic hairs became dark fronds which rippled towards the surface, and then her cunt would rise up again as the waters receded.

Dawn began soaping herself, lazily caressing her superb breasts, her hands gliding down over her sleek body towards her crotch, her eyes closing once more as her fingertips touched her twat – and the film slowly faded into nothingness . . .

'Subtle?' I said, as my own fingers lingered over my vagina.

'Too subtle,' said Richard.

'That was good,' I said, which was true. I was surprised how well made it had been. 'I thought it was very erotic.'

'It was when I was at my peak.'

'I guessed that. Why don't you make another?'

'No reason why not, I suppose. It's been a while since I did one, so maybe I should try it again.' Richard nodded, gazing at the blank screen as he considered the idea. 'But where could I find the right girl . . .?'

I lay in the bath, luxuriously soaping my boobs, fingertips slowly circling my dilated nipples.

Richard was a few feet away, the video camera aimed at my slippery nude body.

Then I leaned forward and I lifted my right leg as if to wash it, but the real reason was to raise my pubis higher out of the water, spreading my legs to give the camera a better view of my cunt. I'd earlier considered shaving my pubic hairs on screen and in close-up. For the sake of my art, anything . . .

But if Richard made a camera error, there could be no second take. Maybe next time. I decided that for my first film it was sufficient to sensuously caress my naked body in the bath, finally pulling the plug and allowing the water to drain away and reveal me totally nude.

I'd watched all of the tapes Richard had previously made, or all of the ones which he admitted to making, and they were basically the same: girl removes her clothes, then takes a bath or a shower or lies down naked on her bed.

'If you've got a good formula,' he said, 'stick to it.'

'But it can't have been a good formula,' I told him, 'because you didn't stick to it. You stopped making them.'

'I didn't make enough money.'

'If you'd made them differently, you might have done.'

'I should have made fuck films, you mean? But I've no interest in that. I'd get jealous of all the studs with their enormous pricks. Eroticism is far more than nudity, far more than fucking. Sex films don't turn me on. The only cock I want to see in a girl's mouth is my own.'

'I'm not talking about that,' I said. 'I meant that you probably got bored making the same film each time. A good-looking girl stripping off all her clothes? That's great – once or twice. But you have to vary the formula.'

'With one girl? How? Have her with a vibrator up her cunt?'

'All your films have been very voyeuristic.'

Richard laughed. 'Isn't that the idea?'

'Yeah, of course. But it's always as if the girl doesn't know the camera is watching her. Instead, you could have her undressing for the camera, knowing that she's not all alone. Like a stripper who takes off her clothes more suggestively because she has an audience, I think the girls in your films should be deliberately provocative rather than innocent. They should constantly tease, be undressing for the camera not for themselves.'

'Maybe,' said Richard, and he shrugged. 'Is that what you want to do if I film you?'

'Maybe,' I said, and I also shrugged. 'I remember what you originally said, about the way that men look at girls and imagine what they're like naked. I get that all the time, I suppose most girls do. Sitting at the checkout in the supermarket, every guy undressing me with his eyes.'

'Who can blame them?'

'I'd like to reverse the formula.'

'So that you're naked in the supermarket?'

'No.' I paused, thinking about Richard's suggestion. 'But that's an idea. What I meant was that instead of me stripping off, I start naked and then get dressed.'

Richard shook his head. 'It won't work.'

I had certain persuasive techniques, however, which brought Richard around to my way of thinking – and so we made the video that started with me naked in the bath.

By then we were living together. I was already spending most of my free time with Richard, and it saved a lot more time when I moved in. Instead of travelling to and from Richard's place, I could do more fucking. Soon after, I also gave up my job at the supermarket and began working for Richard. Because I lived above the shop, he was able to keep the place open whenever he was out doing other things.

The main reason that the shop hadn't been open all the time, I soon discovered, was that Richard had lost interest in it. He was always starting things, never finishing them. For a while he would be totally enthusiastic about his latest venture, but no matter how successful, he was easily bored and very soon another interest would take over.

I knew this would happen to me sooner or

later, and probably sooner. His initial passion would burn out, but while it lasted we'd have a great time together. When it was over, then it was over, and that was okay by me because I had no long-term interest in Richard.

His movies were no different from everything else. They had shown a lot of potential, but he'd become bored and so given up on them. He needed some incentive to make another, and I was that incentive. Like all males, Richard considered he was the dominant part of our relationship, but he also liked it when I was in control – either being on top while we fucked, or calling the shots when he filmed my video.

After climbing from the bath, the camera followed me as I went into the bedroom. I remained naked and deliberately hadn't dried my body, leaving it speckled with drops of water. My flesh was damp and pink, as though I'd been sweating with sexual exertion.

Richard filmed my reflection as I oiled my body, my palms lovingly stroking my breasts. Because of the mirror he could film two of me, see me naked from both the front and rear, my boobs swaying and my buttocks taut as I leaned forward over the dressing table. The camera angle was also my idea.

In his earlier films, the girls had never been completely naked for very long before taking a shower or climbing into bed. But while doing my make-up I could remain nude for quite a while. My intention was to make it appear that the girl in the film – myself – was getting ready to go out on a date, to go out and fuck . . .

She would begin the film naked and remain so

while putting on her lipstick and mascara and combing her hair. Then she'd pull on her sexy undies, and the viewer would know that later she'd be stripping off all her clothes again. Even if this wasn't shown on screen, the person watching could use their imagination. The story wasn't over even when the tape ended, as was the case in all of Richard's other films, when once the girl was naked, that was it.

'How about a close-up of my mouth while I'm putting on my lipstick?' I suggested.

'Yes,' said Richard, as he twisted the camera lens.

'And can I use your cock?'

'Wait till we've finished this scene.'

'I mean as part of this scene,' I said. 'Put the camera on the tripod. I'm holding the lipstick at the very edge of the frame, or it seems that it's lipstick. But really it's your knob. I push back the foreskin and rub the glans across my lips. We'll first have to make it all red with lipstick. Then your cock goes out of view again, and everyone watching thinks *Was that really a prick?*'

'They freeze-frame and know it was real,' said Richard.

'No, they'll think it's too small to be a cock!'

'And I suppose you also want me to ejaculate over your face so you can pretend it's moisturising cream?'

'That's an idea!'

'No. No cock in this film. I told you I don't make that kind of movie. It doesn't interest me.'

There was no point in arguing. He was the one with the camera; he'd only film what he wanted.

Richard had already told me that a film where a

girl seductively stripped off her clothes was always far more erotic and exciting than one in which she fucked and sucked. This seemed reasonable enough at the time; but I later realised it wasn't necessarily the case.

There were so many bad fuck films, where the camera was simply pointing at a guy and a girl – or a guy and two girls, or two guys and a girl, or three girls, two vibrators and a teddy bear. Then they were left to get on with it, and it frequently seemed that it was no more than a job, something which had to be endured rather than enjoyed. Such movies provided convincing evidence that fucking could never be a spectator sport.

In such cases, Richard was right: seeing one girl taking off her clothes could be far more arousing than watching an orgy. (And I hoped that a film where a girl put her clothes on could be equally as stimulating . . .)

But there were also, I was to discover, numerous really great fuck films. The kind of movies which gave the viewer as much sexual pleasure as the people on screen. I liked to think that all of the erotic films which I've made fall into that category. Or almost; I had such a great time and so many orgasms while making them, it was impossible that anyone could have enjoyed watching my movies as much as I enjoyed filming them.

Who did I make my films for? Myself!

I also had an orgasm during my very first movie. Richard had rejected my idea of using his knob as a lipstick, but I kept thinking of his cock sliding across my lips and into my mouth. While he filmed a close-up of my face as I put on some real lipstick, I slid my hand down towards my crotch and started stroking my labia and fingering my clit.

As always, I was very excited by the camera's voyeuristic gaze, and throughout the filming I'd kept looking into the lens. Richard told me not to, but I ignored him. I wasn't pretending that I was alone; I wanted to make it apparent that I knew I was being watched – and that I enjoyed being watched.

And while he filmed my face, capturing my image in the mirror, I was slowly masturbating. Richard had no idea what I was doing, because his whole attention was focused on what he could see through the viewfinder. I put eyeshadow on with my right hand, while my left hand manipulated my cunt. He filmed me as I came, and only by a tremendous effort of will was I able to suppress every outward sign of my rapturous climax.

Already I was a great actress . . .!

The rest of that scene consisted of me putting on my exotic underwear: the crotchless panties, the peep-hole bra, the suspender belt and seamed stockings.

The final scene showed a man taking out his wallet, handing over several notes. All that could be seen of the girl – of me – was her hand, accepting the cash. The camera drew away, showing another man standing in line, also waiting to pay the girl. Then I came into view. I was working. In the checkout in the supermarket.

This part of the movie had been filmed first, on my last day at work. I'd already figured out the structure of the film by then; having seen so much television, I was a real expert on plot techniques.

The film was a sex fantasy, because I knew that while at the supermarket I'd been a sex fantasy for countless men. They'd queued to pay for their shopping, and while waiting in line the most interesting thing to look at was me. And while they looked, they stripped off my clothes, imagining what lay beneath my supermarket overall.

And when they watched the video, they knew.

That was my first film, and I called it *Sex Slut*.

CHAPTER THIRTEEN

I thought that *Sex Slut* was wonderful – and I thought that I was wonderful.

'Okay,' said Richard, 'now what?'

'Let's make another,' I said. 'I've got another great idea, but it will need some special video tricks.'

'I'm talking about this one. What are we going to do with it?'

I hadn't thought as far as that. For me, just making the movie was enough.

'Sell it?'

Richard shook his head. 'Who to? Television?' He laughed. 'There's no market for ten minutes of a girl putting her clothes on.'

'Ten minutes, was that all?'

'By the time it was edited down, yes.'

'I'm naked for at least nine of those ten minutes.'

Richard shrugged. He probably didn't have any plans for the video. He'd made it just to keep me happy – and in return I'd made him very happy. Neither was I really bothered what happened. The film was made, I'd enjoyed doing it, and that was more than enough for me. Making it was art, selling it was commerce. But now that I'd begun, I wanted to make another film.

'Want something else?' asked Richard.

'Yeah, what?'

He stood up and went to collect another cassette. Removing *Sex Slut* from the machine, he slid in the new video.

'This,' he said. 'I only just got hold of it; I haven't seen it yet.'

Since living with Richard, we'd seen a lot of videos together, but I could tell that this was going to be something different. Even before it began, I suspected what kind of tape it was. And I was right: it was a fuck film.

I'd never seen a porno movie before, and for some reason I expected it would be very amateurish. But it was far better than many television programmes. They probably hadn't spent too much money making it, but the production values were excellent. There were proper credits, a soundtrack, some very interesting camera angles and complex tracking shots. The dialogue wasn't very inspired, however, and I had some trouble trying to work out the plot – until I realised that there wasn't one, and that it didn't really matter what they said to each other.

From the costumes which were worn it was evident that the film was meant to be set in the past, although there was no real consistency in the clothing, which varied between the styles of a hundred to five hundred years ago. But the outfits were soon discarded, and the cast got on with what they had to do: they fucked and sucked each other in every possible combination and permutation.

The only people I'd seen fuck on video had been Richard and myself, and I thought that we'd covered everything that two people could do to one another. We probably had, but the addition of extra cocks and extra cunts multiplied the potential sexual configurations beyond all belief.

Not only had I never seen anything like it, I'd never even imagined anything like it. Even Lynn's stories hadn't prepared me for what I saw on screen. I was aware that her sexy exploits were mostly fantasy, but this was for real. The film was all made up, of course. But the fucking wasn't. That was really real.

And it was all filmed in such explicit detail, which was something Richard had only rarely managed to do. One time he'd knelt above me, the camera aimed down at my face, zooming in for a graphic close-up as I sucked on his cock. He'd wanted to film himself spunking into my mouth, to watch his sperm speckle my tongue, but I'd had a better idea and aimed his squirting knob at the camera lens – then licked it clean.

On screen now, everything was in perfect focus. A thick tool slid into a slick twat, and the image of the glans parting the moist labia filled the television. Wet vaginas were licked, the tongues being both male and female. A beautiful blonde girl smiled at the camera, which moved in to focus on her lips, and she opened her mouth to welcome a pulsing penis.

I watched in total fascination. My heart beat faster with excitement, and my body was damp; with sweat. It was almost as if I was there, and I wished that I could be . . .

Richard wasn't watching. At first he picked up

a magazine and started reading, but then he left the room. Although he'd claimed he wasn't interested in such films, I still couldn't believe it. I guessed that he'd watched the tape before.

I remained where I was, my eyes locked on the TV screen, gazing at all the gorgeous naked flesh which writhed together in a passionate orgy of tongues and twats, cocks and come.

Another scene began, in which one of the maids carried a crystal decanter and two wine glasses into the dining room. She was one of the three girls in the film. The other two were brunettes, but it was the blonde who had the shaven pubis. There were also two guys in the movie, the younger one with mermaids tattooed on his forearms.

The two men were sitting at either end of a huge table. While the maid poured the wine, one of the men reached behind and raised her long dress, doing it slowly as if she would not notice. She was wearing nothing beneath the dress. With a sudden pull, the garment was gone and she was naked to the waist.

She turned and the man gazed at her hairless twat, then beckoned to his companion. Between them, they removed the rest of the blonde's clothes and lifted her on to the table. She laughed, making no attempt to resist. The camera focused upon her smooth cunt.

The men were also laughing. There was some dialogue, but by now I'd learned to filter out everything that was said. I would have turned down the volume completely, except I'd have missed out on all the sighs and moans of gratification and orgasm, the noise of tongues on wet flesh, the sounds of dick sliding between labia.

The other two girls came into the room, also dressed as maids. They didn't remain dressed for long. Seeing what was happening, they started pulling off the men's clothes while the two guys pulled off theirs. In a matter of seconds, everyone was totally naked. The five of them then did what they were there for: they fucked, they sucked.

They fucked in pairs, in threesomes. They sucked while being sucked by someone who was being fucked by someone who was being sucked by someone who was being fucked. Whatever a cock could do to a girl, it was done. Whatever a female tongue could do to either male or female, the three girls did it.

Five glistening nude bodies rolled and writhed upon the table, and because of the way their flesh was so tightly intertwined it was often difficult to make out which cock belonged to which guy or whose cunt was being tongued so lovingly. Which girl was licking whose knob while it slid into whose twat? It didn't really matter, I supposed.

The two guys were busy with one of the brunettes. She had a cock in her cunt, another in her mouth. The blonde and the other brunette were meanwhile licking each other's vulvas, and it was this mutual oral adoration which interested me much more. I wondered what it would be like to have a girl perform cunnilingus on me. Could a girl tongue twat better than a man? It was possible, because she was aware what she liked having done to her own body and therefore more likely to know how to pleasure another female.

And I also wondered what it would be like to taste another girl's cunt . . .

As I dreamed of clit licking, the five switched their positions yet again. The brunettes directed their mouths to the tattooed guy's cock, which was plenty large enough for both of them. One drew the head between her lips, and the other licked his balls. While this was going on, his own tongue was darting in and out of the blonde's hairless twat. She was sucking off the second guy, while his hands were busy finger-fucking the other two girls.

Then another girl started licking at the blonde's smooth cunt, drawing her swollen clit into her mouth, caressing her vaginal lips with her fingertips.

Something didn't make sense here, and I started counting the naked bodies. There were now six of them. Another nude girl had joined the group. She hadn't been in the film before, but she was the one whose tongue and fingers were teasing the hairless twat. The blonde's whole body writhed in a frenzy of passion, and she cried out as she climaxed. I was certain that she wasn't faking.

As she came, she released the cock which was halfway down her throat, and the new girl immediately took possession. She straddled the guy, guiding his knob deep into her cunt, and started to ride him. The blonde started to stroke her tits, then began kissing her.

Her hair was jet-black, waist-length – and I suddenly recognised her. It was Dawn, the girl who had been in the first video which Richard had shown me. She was the one who'd worn the white suit and high-heeled boots, then removed them, stripped off her undies, and taken a bath.

What was she doing in the movie? Was this another of Richard's films, one he'd kept secret until now?

I had no doubt that the girl was Dawn, although she looked slightly different. Her hair was longer than it had been, and so obviously some time had passed. That was the difference, I realised. She was a few years older than in Richard's video. No longer a teenager, she was probably in her mid-twenties, but her body was still perfect.

Because I was so surprised, I missed out on some of the action. But whatever film I saw, I always hated running back the tape because it broke the continuity. I kept watching.

Dawn lifted herself free of the guy's cock. It seemed he was about to ejaculate, and I couldn't help but admire his stamina in having lasted so long. Dawn moved close to the imminent eruption, and I thought he was going to cream over her face. Instead, there was a wine glass in her hand and she held it close to the man's prick.

Then his spunk began to spurt, silver streams splashing into the crystal glass – and Dawn caught every drop.

Raising the glass as if in a toast, she tilted it above her face, and the creamy drops of semen dripped down, some falling between her lips, others splattering around her mouth. Now the blonde was by her side, her face pressed close, sharing the unique spray which showered over them. When no more sperm would fall from the glass, they dipped their fingers inside, scooping up what remained. Dawn sucked at the blonde's come-laden index finger, and she greedily lapped the warm drops that Dawn had collected.

Their tongues licked at one another's face, drawing in every last atom of spunk which speckled their skin. Then they kissed. The camera moved even closer. Their tongues caressed, sharing the final exquisite taste of semen between them.

That was how the film ended, or almost. The credits came up while the two girls continued passionately kissing and fondling one another. It was almost as if the movie didn't stop, that it continued although the viewer was unable to watch, because by the time the picture faded the two of them had started licking at each other's cunt.

A MurFylm by Murphy, read the final credit, while the blonde tongued Dawn's clit, and then the screen went blank.

'That was . . . amazing,' I said. I was talking to myself, because Richard still hadn't returned. But it was true, I was amazed. Amazed and thrilled and very excited.

If Richard had been there, I'd have gone down on him immediately. What I would have liked was a glass to catch his spunk, the most potent and exotic liqueur there was.

But he was nowhere around, and a girl has to do what a girl has to do . . .

I used my fingers to bring myself off, and because I was in such a state of sexual arousal it didn't take very long before I achieved a wonderful climax.

Richard was down in the shop, repairing an

audio cassette deck.

'You missed a good film,' I told him. By now I was convinced that he had seen the tape, and he'd shown it to me because of Dawn. But I wasn't sure what he was trying to tell me.

He shrugged.

'Dawn was in it,' I told him.

'Who?'

'Dawn. The girl in your first film. Looks like she's become a star.'

'Good.'

'Did you ever fuck her?'

He shrugged again. 'Maybe.'

'Or maybe not,' I said. 'But definitely not on film.'

'No.' Richard looked at me for the first time. 'Ours was purely a professional arrangement. She wanted to be a model, I had a video camera. As long as the camera was between us, she was willing to take off her clothes. I should have asked to film us fucking, because she'd probably have agreed.'

'Why did you show me the film?'

'To let you know what we're up against. We can't compete. One naked girl compared to *that* . . .'

'We can do better than that,' I said. 'I want to make a video about a girl who fantasises about another girl. Have you ever thought about the closeness of the words "image" and "imagination"? This is what the movie is all about. The girl is sexually attracted to her image on the other side of the mirror. We'll call the film *Sweet Lips*. . .'

*

I stood naked in front of the mirror, studying my nude reflection.

My image stared back at me, and we both leaned towards each other. Our lips almost met and our boobs nearly rubbed together. The only thing separating us was the mirror itself.

It was a huge mirror, as high as I was, and I could see every detail of my perfect nude other self. The mirror was standing vertically against the wall, and now I took it down and laid it on the floor.

Supporting myself on my hands and knees, I gazed down at the girl who had been my best friend for as long as I could remember.

The camera looked up from my reflection's point of view, filming me through the piece of glass on which I really knelt. I moved closer to the lens, rubbing my whole body over the glass, sliding my pubis and tits across the cold surface.

Then the camera angle changed, and again it was a mirror that I was spread upon. It was as if I were lying above myself, stroking my body against my image.

There was a close-up on my lips, kissing the mirror, mouth against reflected mouth.

And then my reflection kissed me, lips pressing hard against mine, tongue flickering across to meet my own . . .

This was no mere image. The camera drew back. I was still lying above my other self, but my reflection had come to life.

We kissed passionately, caressing one another, erotically embracing, rolling over and over and over together, finally able to touch after being so very close yet so far apart for so many years.

We stroked one another, fingers sensuously exploring the bodies which we knew as intimately as our own. Our mouths followed our fingertips, tasting instead of touching, sucking at our erect nipples, then moving lower, lower, down and further down, aiming towards the hearts of our sexuality.

Finally our mouths met our cunts, doing what we could not do for ourselves, tongues darting in and out of our throbbing twats.

It was absolute paradise.

There was a lot of trickery in the film; all the effects to make my other self come alive, the camera angles which only showed my face. My face played two roles, my body acted but one.

The role of Sweet Lips was taken by Dawn, and she was truly magnificent. Her body was soft and supple, sweet and splendid.

She sucked my cunt better than it had ever been sucked before, her own twat tasted truly delicious, and my orgasm was absolutely beautiful, going on and on and forever on, raising me higher and higher and eternally higher.

And there's more, so much more that I have to tell. I haven't yet revealed how I met Dawn and began working with Murphy, but I'll leave all of that until next time . . .